austenland

shannon hale

BLOOMSBURY
LONDON • NEW DELHI • NEW YORK • SYDNEY

First published in Great Britain 2013

Copyright © 2007 by Shannon Hale

The moral right of the author has been asserted

Bloomsbury Publishing Plc
50 Bedford Square
London WC1B 3DP

www.bloomsbury.com

Bloomsbury Publishing, London, New Delhi, New York and Sydney
A CIP catalogue record for this book is available from the British Library

ISBN 978 1 4088 4009 2

Printed and bound in Great Britain by CPI Group (UK) Ltd, Croydon CR0 4YY

prologue

IT IS A TRUTH UNIVERSALLY acknowledged that a thirty-something woman in possession of a satisfying career and fabulous hairdo must be in want of very little, and Jane Hayes, pretty enough and clever enough, was certainly thought to have little to distress her. There was no husband, but those weren't necessary anymore. There were boyfriends, and if they came and went in a regular stream of mutual dissatisfaction—well, that was the way of things, wasn't it?

But Jane had a secret. By day, she bustled and luncheoned and e-mailed and over-timed and just-in-timed, but sometimes, when she had the time to slip off her consignment store pumps and lounge on her hand-me-down sofa, she dimmed the lights, turned on her nine-inch television, and acknowledged what was missing.

Sometimes, she watched *Pride and Prejudice*.

You know, the BBC double DVD version, starring Colin Firth as the delicious Mr. Darcy and that comely, busty English actress as the Elizabeth Bennet we had imagined all along. Jane watched and rewatched the part where Elizabeth and Mr. Darcy look at each other over the piano, and there's that *zing*, and her face softens, and he smiles, his chest heaving as though he'd breathe in the sight of her, and his eyes are glistening so that you'd almost think he'd cry . . . Ah!

Each time, Jane's heart banged, her skin chilled, and she clamped down on the distracting ache in her gut with a bowl of something naughty, like Cocoa Pebbles. That night she would dream of gentlemen in Abraham Lincoln hats, and then in the morning laugh at herself and toy with the idea of hauling those DVDs and all her Austen books to the second-hand store.

Of course, she never did.

That pesky movie version was the culprit. Sure, Jane had first read *Pride and Prejudice* when she was sixteen, read it a dozen times since, and read the other Austen novels at least twice, except *Northanger Abbey* (of course). But it wasn't until the BBC put a face on the story that those gentlemen in tight breeches had stepped out of her reader's imagination and into her nonfiction hopes. Stripped of Austen's funny, insightful, biting narrator, the movie became a pure romance. And *Pride and Prejudice* was the most stunning, bite-your-hand romance ever, the kind that stared straight into Jane's soul and made her shudder.

It was embarrassing. She didn't really want to talk about it. So let's move on.

1 year ago

JANE'S MOTHER, SHIRLEY, CAME TO visit and brought along Great-Aunt Carolyn. It was an awkward gathering, and in the lapses of conversation, Jane could hear dead leaves crack as they hit her apartment floor. She loved her houseplants, but keeping them alive seemed beyond her skills.

"Really, Jane, I don't know how you survive here," said Shirley, picking the brittle leaves from among the sallow green ones. "We had a near-death experience in your coffin-of-an-elevator, didn't we Carolyn, dear? I'm sure your poor aunt wants to relax, but it's like a sauna in here and not a moment of silence—traffic, car alarms, sirens nonstop. Are you sure your windows aren't open?"

"It's Manhattan, Mom. That's just how it is."

"Well, I don't know about that." She took a scolding stance, hand on hip. The sixty-year-old wood floor grunted beneath her feet. "I just picked up Carolyn from her apartment, and sitting in her front room it was so blessedly quiet I could have sworn we were in the country."

That's because money buys thick windows, Jane thought.

"Never mind. Tell me, how's your . . ."

Please don't say it! Jane thought. Don't ask about my love life!

". . . friend Molly doing?"

"Oh, Molly. Yeah, she's great, working freelance for the paper since she had the twins. Molly and I have been friends since the sixth grade," Jane explained to Carolyn, who sat in her wheelchair by the front door.

Carolyn had as many wrinkles in her face as there are ridges in a fingerprint, not just around her eyes and on her brow, but delicate folds rippling across her thin cheeks. She returned a blank stare then tweaked it slightly, an intimation of rolling her eyes. Jane didn't know if it was pointed or conspiratorial, so she pretended not to notice.

She hadn't seen Carolyn since she was twelve, at her grandmother's funeral. It had struck her as odd that when her mother came into the city, Shirley had insisted on including Carolyn in their lunch plans. But from the hungry, significant looks her mother kept pushing on her, Jane could guess—the old woman was getting older, and Shirley wanted to make an impression, a last bid for the remains of the seafood fortune. No doubt picking up Jane at her apartment rather than meeting at the restaurant was a ploy to show Carolyn her great-niece's shameful living conditions.

"Shall we skedaddle?" asked Jane, eager to get the meddling over with.

"Yes, sweetheart, let me just fix your hair."

And Jane, age thirty-two, followed her mother into the bathroom and submitted herself to the slicking and spraying and twisting. No matter her age, whenever her mother did her hair, Jane felt exactly seven years old. But she let her mom go to town, because Shirley "Miss French Twist 1967" Hayes could only find true tranquillity in a well-placed do.

"Be sure you *listen*, dear," said Shirley, delivering her hushed, urgent lecture on How to Impress the Elderly. "They love that. Ask her about her childhood and let her go on, if she's so inclined. At this point in her life, memories are all she has left, poor lamb."

When they emerged from the bathroom, Carolyn wasn't where they had left her. Jane rushed into the next room, jolted with a nightmare of a wheelchair bumping down the stairs (and with it an unnerving flashback of watching *The Changeling* at her eleventh birthday slumber party). But there was Carolyn by the window, leaning over to tug a floor plant into the yellow square of sunlight. Jane heard a *thwack* as her *Pride and Prejudice* DVDs fell from their arboreal hideaway and onto the floor.

Jane felt herself flush. Carolyn smiled, her uncountable cheek wrinkles gathered into a few deeper ones.

Really, so what if she had seen the DVDs? A lot of people owned them. Why should she hide them? She didn't hide her copy of *Arrested Development: Season 1* or *Yoga for Dummies*. Still, something in Carolyn's smile made her feel as though she stood there in her underwear. Dirty underwear.

At the restaurant when Shirley left to powder her proverbial nose, Jane did her best to pretend she was not the least bit uncomfortable. A minute of silence passed. She plowed her garden salad with a fork, weeding out the arugula.

"It's been a warm autumn," she offered.

"You're wondering if I saw it," Carolyn said. Some voices get hard and tight with age, some rough like broken glass. Her voice was soft, sand beat by waves till it's as fine as powdered sugar.

"Saw what?" Jane asked halfheartedly.

"He is a devil, that Mr. Darcy. But you wouldn't hide him in a houseplant if you didn't have a guilty conscience. That tells me you're not idly daydreaming. You're past thirty, not married, not dating—if your mother's gossip and the photos in your apartment tell the truth. And it all comes down to that story. You're obsessed."

Jane laughed. "I am not obsessed."

But really she was.

"Hm. You're blushing. Tell me, what is it about that story that's so intoxicating?"

Jane gulped down her water and glanced over her shoulder toward the ladies' room, making sure her mother wasn't returning. "Besides being witty and funny and maybe the best novel ever written, it's also the most perfect romance in all of literature and nothing in life can ever measure up, so I spend my life limping in its shadow."

Carolyn stared, as if waiting for more. Jane thought she'd said enough already.

"It is a lovely novel," Carolyn said, "but you weren't concealing a paperback in your plant. I've seen the movie. I know who Colin Firth is, my dear. And I think I know what you've put your life on hold to wait for."

"Listen, I don't actually believe I can somehow end up married to Mr. Darcy. I just . . . nothing in real life feels as right as . . . oh, never mind, I don't want you believing your great-niece is living in a fantasyland."

"Are you?"

Jane forced a smile. "Warm autumn, isn't it?"

Carolyn pressed her lips together so they were as wrinkled as her cheeks. "How's your love life?"

"I'm on the wagon."

"Is that so? Giving up at age thirty-two. Hm. May I hazard a guess?" Carolyn leaned forward, her silky voice easing between the sounds of clattering plates and too-hardy businessmen laughter. "Things aren't working out so well, and each time the men in your life disappoint, you let Mr. Darcy in a little bit more. Perhaps you've come to the point where you're so attached to the idea of that scoundrel, you won't be satisfied with anything less."

An olive stuck to the piece of lettuce on Jane's fork, and when she tried to flick it off, it flew over the table and tapped a waiter in the butt. Jane scowled. Certainly, her list of ex-boyfriends was impressively pathetic. And there was that dream she'd had a few weeks ago—she'd been dressed in a ragged wedding gown (à la Miss Havisham of *Great Expectations* fame), dancing alone in a dark house, waiting for Mr. Darcy to come for her. When she awoke with a sharp intake of breath, the dream had been still too raw and terrifying to laugh at. In fact, she still couldn't.

"Maybe I am batty," Jane said.

"I remember you, Jane." Carolyn had pale blue eyes like denim washed too often. "I remember sitting in that gazebo with you by the lake after my sister's, your grandmother's, funeral. I remember you weren't afraid to say how during the service you couldn't help wondering what might be for lunch and was that wrong? Did that mean that you didn't love your grandma enough? Your voice, your little girl questions took some of the sting out of my grief. You're too honest to let yourself get duped like this."

Jane nodded. "That day, you were wearing a lace collar. I thought it was elegant."

"My late husband bought me that dress. It was my favorite." Carolyn refolded her napkin, smoothing the edge with slightly shaky hands. "Harold and I had a miserable marriage. He didn't talk much and was busy with work. I got bored and was rich enough to date delectable young men on the side. After a time, Harold fooled around, too, mostly to hurt me, I think. It wasn't until I was too old to attract the playboys anymore that I turned to the man next to me and realized how much I loved his face. We had two blissful years together before his heart took him out. I

7

was such a fool, Jane. I couldn't see what was real until time had washed away everything else." She was matter-of-fact, the pain behind the words worn out long ago.

"I'm sorry."

"Hmph. It'd be better to be sorry for yourself. I'm old and rich, and people let me say whatever I want. So here it is. Figure out what is real for you. No use leaning on someone else's story all your life. You know, that book did Austen herself no good—died a spinster."

"I know." The thought had haunted Jane many times, and it was a favorite weapon of anti-Austen enthusiasts.

"Not that there's anything wrong with spinsters," Carolyn said, patting the fragile folds in her neck.

"Of course not. Spinster is just an archaic term for 'career-minded.'"

"Listen, sweetie, my story's told. I've had my dancing days, and I'm facing my own The End. But sky and stars know how your story will turn out. So go make your happily-ever-after happen." Her voice had a Little League coach enthusiasm. It was sweetly patronizing. Time to change the subject. Very nonchalantly.

"Why don't you tell me about your childhood, Aunt Carolyn?"

Carolyn laughed, soft as room-temperature butter. "Tell you about my childhood, and just in the nick of time. Well, don't mind if I do. I was a limper from the time I could walk. Our folks were poor and your grandma and I shared a bed that leaned to one side, though I can't be sure if that bed was the cause . . ."

When Shirley returned from the restroom, Carolyn was quoting the price of milk when she was a child, and Shirley gave her daughter an approving smile. Thanks be she hadn't overheard the batty-great-niece part of the conversation. Her mother was practical from her robust eyeglass frames to her thick-heeled shoes, and no daughter of hers would dally about in a fantasyland.

And Jane was eager to agree. Seriously, a thirty-something woman shouldn't be daydreaming about a fictional character in a two-hundred-year-old world to the point where it interfered with her very real and much more important life and relationships. Of course she shouldn't.

Jane crunched down on a piece of arugula.

6 months ago

GREAT-AUNT CAROLYN PASSED AWAY.

"And you're in the will, dear!" her mother said, calling from Vermont. "Apparently our last-minute lunch did the trick. The lawyer will be in touch. Call me the moment you learn the amount!"

Jane hung up and sat down, forcing herself not to think about the will, spending a few moments with the thought of the woman who'd loved Harold's face, who'd wasted three decades of loving, who'd ripped open Jane's chest and laid out what she saw. She had not known Carolyn well enough to grieve, only to feel softened, mystified by the idea of death.

And yet, Carolyn had thought of Jane enough to scratch her name into the will. What *would* she leave a near-stranger relative? Carolyn had a large family so the amount couldn't be much, but then again the rumors of her great-aunt's wealth were legendary. Enough to move her into an apartment with air-conditioning? Enough to retire?

Jane balked at that thought. It wasn't so much that she loved her job—it wasn't bad work, doing graphic design at the magazine, but it was, you know, a *job*. She couldn't knock such a nice piece of stability, somewhere to go every day, something (unlike men) that didn't rip the rug out from under her and send her sprawling. But on the subway ride to the attorney's, Jane wondered, if she were tempted with a huge sum, would she fold? Would she quit her job and buy a house in the Hamptons and adopt a miniature poodle named Porridge who peed on the carpet?

These questions and alternate names for the poodle kept her mind busy as she traveled up into the law firm's sleek gray building, up into the conservative burgundy and tan office, down into a stuffed leather chair to hear the extraordinarily pale lawyer say, "You're not rich."

"What?"

"In fact, she didn't leave you any money at all." His every blink was slow and deliberate, reminding Jane of a frog. "People often hope, so I like to get that out up front."

Jane laughed uneasily. "Oh, I wasn't thinking that."

"Of course." The attorney sat down and sorted through a stack of papers with no wasted movement. He was saying something in lawyer-ese, but Jane was distracted. She was trying to figure out what besides the measured blinking made him seem so amphibious. His taut, shiny complexion, she decided. And his eyes being so wide apart. And his salad green tone. (Okay, he wasn't actually green, but the rest was true.)

He was still talking. "Our client was . . . eclectic . . . in her will. She made purchases for a few friends and family members and left the bulk of her money to charities. For you, she arranged a vacation."

He handed her a glossy, oversized pamphlet. On the cover was a photograph of a large manor house. A man in jacket, cravat, and breeches, and a woman in an empire-waist dress and bonnet were walking in the foreground. They seemed awfully content. Jane's hands went cold.

She read the elegantly inserted text.

Pembrook Park, Kent, England. Enter our doors as a house guest come to stay three weeks, enjoying the country manners and hospitality—a tea visit, a dance or two, a turn in the park, an unexpected meeting with a certain gentleman, all culminating with a ball and perhaps something more . . .

Here, the Prince Regent still rules a carefree England. No scripts. No written endings. A holiday no one else can offer you.

"I don't get it."

"It's an all-inclusive, three-week vacation in England. From what I gather, you dress up and pretend to be someone in the year 1816." The attorney handed her a packet. "It also comes with a first-class plane ticket. The vacation is nonrefundable, my client saw to that. But if you do need cash, you could exchange the first-class airfare for economy class and pocket the change. I make such suggestions whenever I can. I like to be helpful."

Jane hadn't looked away from the pamphlet. The man and woman in the photo held her gaze like a magician's swaying watch. She hated them and adored them, longed to be that woman but needed to stay firmly in New York City in the present day and pretend she had no such odd fantasies. No one guessed her thoughts, not her mother, not her closest friends. But Great-Aunt Carolyn had known.

"Pocket the change," she said distractedly.

"Just make certain you report it to the IRS."

"Right." Seemed odd, that Carolyn would point out this flaw in her poor, pathetic great-niece and then send her right into the belly of the beast. Jane groaned. "I'm hopeless."

"What was that?"

"Um, did I say that out loud? Anyway, I'm *not* hopeless, that's the problem. I'm too hopeful, if anything." She sat up, leaning against his desk. "If I were to tell you my first dozen boyfriend stories, you'd call me screwy for ever going out with anyone again. But I have! I'm so thick-headed it's taken me this long to give up on men, but I can't give up completely, you know? So I . . . I channel all my hope into an idea, to someone who can't reject me because he isn't real!"

The lawyer straightened a stack of papers. "I think I should clarify, Miss Hayes, that I did not mean to flirt. I am a happily married man."

Jane gaped. "Uh, of course you are. My mistake. I'll just be going now." She grabbed her purse and split.

The elevator dropped her back at street level, and even after stepping through the doors, the ground still felt as though it were falling away under her feet. She fell/walked all the way back to work and into her gray rollerchair.

Todd the manager was at her cubicle the moment her chair squeaked.

"How you doin', Jane?" he asked in his oft-affected pseudo-*Sopranos* accent.

"Fine."

She stared. He had a new haircut. His white blond hair was now spiked with an incredible amount of pomade that smelled of raspberries, a do that could only be carried off with true success by a fifteen-year-old boy wielding an impressive and permanent glare. Todd was grinning. And forty-three. Jane wondered if politeness required her to offer a compliment on something glaringly obvious.

"Uh . . . you, your hair is different."

"Hey, girls always notice the hair. Right? Isn't that basically right?"

"I guess I just proved it," she said sadly.

"Super. Hey, listen," he sat on the edge of her desk, "we've got a last-minute addition that needs special attention. It may seem like your basic stock photo array, but don't be fooled! This is for the all-important page sixteen layout. I'd give this one to your basic interns, but I'm choosing you because I think you'd do a super job. What d'you say?"

"Sure thing, Todd."

"Su-per." He gave her two thumbs-up and held them there, smiling, his eyes unblinking. After a few moments, Jane cringed. What did he want her to do? Was she supposed to high-five his thumbs? Touch thumb-pad to thumb-pad? Or did he just leave them there so long for emphasis?

The silence quivered. At last Jane opted for raising her own thumbs in a mirror of the Todd salute.

"All right, my lady Jane." He nodded, still with the thumbs up, and kept them up as he walked away. At least he hadn't asked her out again. Why was it that when she was aching for a man, everyone was married, but when she was giving them up, so many men were so awkwardly single?

As soon as Todd's cologne faded down the hall, Jane Googled Pembrook Park.

There were parks by that name scattered across the United States, but nothing Austen and nothing English. A couple of cryptic mentions in blogs seemed to touch Jane's Pembrook, such as a blogger named tan'n'fun, "Back from Pembrook Park, my second year. Even better than the first, especially the ball . . . but I signed a confidentiality agreement, so that's all I'll say publicly." No Wikipedia article about the elusive locale. No photos. This was the Area 51 of vacation resorts.

She banged her head lightly on the monitor.

The question *Should I go?* limped after her all afternoon. Jane certainly had the vacation hours saved up. She had an impressive benefits package including three weeks off a year, and she rarely went on holiday (note: she used the British word for "vacation" in her thoughts, an early sign that she'd already decided to go).

And besides: *Nonrefundable*. It was a good, solid word, one you couldn't chew, one that only dissolved after sucking slowly.

Jane argued with her thoughts and her thoughts argued back while she searched through stock photo databases for Todd's basically super project. *Search words: smiling woman.* 2,317 results, way too many to scan through. *Narrow search results: smiling businesswoman.* 214 results. *Narrow search results: smiling businesswoman twenties.*

And suddenly, there was Jane's face on her own monitor, as photographed by ex-boyfriend #7, the delinquent artist. She'd stumbled across it before. In her line of work, it was hard not to view every stock photo in the digital empire at least twice. But this was really bad timing. Here she was, dizzy with thoughts of her own stupidity and vulnerability and all other Dr. Phil-ness, and to suddenly confront her own face years younger . . . well, *ick*, an unpleasant reminder that she was just as stupid and vulnerable back then. She hadn't changed. She'd been standing knee-deep in the same romance mud for years and she didn't even care anymore.

The photo array completed and two train rides later, Jane plopped down on Molly's couch in Brooklyn, keeping one eye on the twins battling over blocks, the other eye ensconced in a throw pillow. She held her arm straight up and waved the brochure like a surrender flag. Molly pulled it out of her hand and read it.

"So it's come to this," Molly said.

"Help," Jane squeaked.

Molly nodded. "I don't know, Jane, do you really think you should subject yourself to something like this? . . . *Good job, Jack! Did you stack those blocks all by yourself? You're such a smart boy, my big smart boy* . . . It might make things worse. You just might fade away into a Mr. Darcy Brigadoon for good."

Jane sat up. "So you know how bad I am? The whole Darcy thingie?"

Molly put a hand on her leg. "Honey, I don't blame you. You've had rotten luck with that whole romance sh—uh, crap," she said, amending her diction as she glanced at the kids. Hannah had managed to stick both her fingers into her nostrils and tottered over to Molly to show off her new trick. "*Did you find your nose holes? What a smart girl!* . . . Janie, are you going to get sad if I say this? Should I say this?"

"Say it."

"Okay." A deep breath. "This obsession . . ."

Jane groaned at the word and completely buried her face in the throw pillow.

". . . has been brewing since we were in high school. I used to fantasize about jumping Darcy's bones myself, but you've turned it into a career. You've been forced into it by a train wreck of bad relationships, it's true, but the last couple of years . . ."

"I know, I know," Jane mumbled into the pillow. "I've been freaking out, I sabotaged myself, and I couldn't see it at the time, but I can now, so maybe I'm okay."

Molly paused. "Are you okay?"

Jane shook her head and the pillow with it. "No! I'm spooked I'll do it again. I'm so afraid I'm damaged and castoff-able and unlovable and I'm not even really sure what I'm doing wrong. What should I do, Molly? Please tell me."

"Oh, honey . . ."

"Uh-oh."

Molly cleared her throat and adopted her most gentle tone. "Have you noticed that you refer to any guy you've ever been on a date with as a 'boyfriend'?"

Jane had noticed it. In fact, she'd numbered all her boyfriends from one to thirteen and referred to them in her mind by their number. She was relieved now that she'd never mentioned that part to Molly.

"It's not really normal to do that," Molly said. "It's kind of . . . extreme. Kind of slaps expectation on a relationship before it's begun."

"Uh-huh," was all Jane could muster in response, even to her best friend. This was a raw, pin-poking subject. A couple of years ago, she'd toyed with having a therapist, and though in the end she'd decided she just wasn't a therapy kind of a gal, she did come out of it understanding one thing about herself: At a very young age, she had learned how to love from Austen. And according to her immature understanding at the time, in Austen's world there was no such thing as a fling. Every romance was intended to lead to marriage, every flirtation just a means to find that partner to cling to forever. So for Jane, when each romance ended with hope still attached, it felt as brutal as divorce. Intense much, Jane? Oh yes. But what can you do?

"Jane." Molly rubbed her arm. "You've got so much going on! You don't need this Pembrook Park, and you definitely don't need Mr. Darcy."

"I know. I mean, he's not even real. He's not, he's not, I know he's not, but maybe . . ."

"There's no maybe. He's not real."

Jane groaned. "But I don't want to have to settle."

"You always do. Every single guy you ever dated was a settle."

She sat up. "None of them loved me, did they? Ever. Some of them liked me or I was convenient but . . . Am I truly that pathetic?"

Molly smoothed her hair. "No, of course not," she said, which meant, Yes, but I love you anyway.

"Argh," Jane arghed. "I don't know what to do, I don't trust myself. I mean, how did you ever know for sure that Phillip was the right guy?"

Molly shrugged. It was the same shrug that had twitched in Molly's shoulders at summer camp eighteen years ago when Jane had asked, "Did you eat all my marshmallows?" It was the same shrug Molly had given when Jane adopted the New Wave style in sixth grade and asked, "How do I look?" Molly had forsworn her shifty days in college and declared she'd be a forthright, unashamed woman forever—but here was that bad-penny shrug turning up again.

Jane glared. "Don't you do it, Ms. Molly Andrews-Carrero. What is it? Tell me. How do you know that Phillip is the one?"

Molly picked at some dried spaghetti sauce on her pants. "He . . . he makes me feel like the most beautiful woman in the world, every day of my life."

She'd never admit it, but those words made Jane's tear ducts sting. "Wow. You've never told me that. Why didn't you ever tell me that before?!"

Molly started to shrug, then stopped. "It's not something you tell your single best friend. It'd be like rubbing your nose in the poop of my happiness."

"If I didn't love you, I'd slap you." Jane reconsidered and threw a pillow at Molly's face. "You need to tell me those things, loser. I've got to know what's possible."

Or what's impossible, Jane thought.

"Are you okay?" Molly asked.

"Yes. I am. Because I've decided to give up men entirely."

"Come on, not again. Sweetie—"

"I'm serious this time. I've had it. I know in my bones that I'm never going to find my Phillip, and all this hoping and waiting is killing me." She took a breath. "This is good, Molly. You'll see. Time to embrace spinsterhood. Time to—"

"Watch out!" Molly said, dropping the brochure and jumping up just as Jack placed a full bowl of milk and cereal onto his head like a marvelous dripping hat.

Hannah picked up the glossy paper and handed it to Jane, backing up onto her lap. The little girl felt so cozy and perfect, like warming her hands on a cup of hot chocolate, and with the familiar bliss that came with holding someone else's child, Jane felt that weird ache in her gut, that ugly nudge that told her she might never have one of her own.

"My ovaries are screaming at me," Jane said.

"Sorry, honey!" Molly called from the kitchen.

"Book." Hannah shook the brochure, so they looked at it together.

"There's a house," Jane said. "Where's the man? That's right! And where's the woman? Yep, that'll be me. Did you know that your aunty Jane is a chump? That she secretly wants to be someone else in another time and be loved like a fictional character in a book? And that she loathes this part of herself? Well, no more!"

"The End," said Hannah. She shut the brochure, squirmed off Jane's lap, and set off searching for something more interesting while chanting, "Hippo, hippo."

Jane lay back down, but this time placed the throw pillow *under* her head. Okay, all right, she *would* go. It would be her last hurrah. Like her friend Becky, who'd taken an all-you-can-eat dinner cruise the night before going in for a stomach stapling, Jane was going to have one last live-it-up and then quit men entirely. She'd play out her fantasy, have a staggering good time, and then bury it all for good. No more Darcy. No more men—period. When she got home she'd become a perfectly normal woman, content to be single, happy with her own self.

She'd even throw the DVDs away.

3 weeks and 1 day ago

JANE FLEW COACH TO LONDON and found a black limo (A limo! she thought) waiting for her at Heathrow. The derbied driver opened the door and took her carry-on bag—just a change of clothes, toiletries, and travel entertainment. She was told she wouldn't need anything else once she got to the Park.

"Is it far?" she asked.

"About three hours, ma'am," he said, keeping his eyes on the pavement.

"Another three hours." She tried to think of something witty and British to say. "I already feel like a thrice-used tea bag."

He didn't smile.

"Oh. Um, I'm Jane. What's your name?"

He shook his head. "Not allowed to say."

Of course, she thought, I'm entering Austenland. The servant class is invisible.

Jane spent the drive going over her packet of notes, "Social History of the Regency Period," and felt as though she were cramming for a test in some uninteresting but required college course. It was not like her to come so unprepared, and she admitted to herself that she had shut out the reality of this adventure since the moment she had signed the papers and mailed them back to the frog attorney. Even thinking of it now sent sharp, cold pains shooting down her legs, stirring in her the anxious energy it took to make an end-of-game shot in high school basketball.

There were a lot of notes.

- On meeting, a gentleman is presented to the lady first because it is considered an honor for him to meet her.

- The eldest daughter in the family is called "Miss" plus surname, while any younger daughters are "Miss" plus Christian and surname. For example, Jane, the eldest, was Miss Bennet, while her sister was Miss Elizabeth Bennet.

- Whist is an early form of bridge played by two couples. The rules are . . .

And so on for pages and pages, all irritatingly numbered with Roman numerals. The epilogue was an admonition written by the Pembrook Park proprietress, who bore the unlikely name of Mrs. Wattlesbrook: "It is imperative that these social customs be followed to the letter. For the sake of all our guests, any person who flagrantly disobeys these rules will be asked to leave. Complete immersion in the Regency period is the only way to truly Experience Austen's England."

Hours later, when the nameless driver stopped the car and opened her door, Jane found herself in the quaint, green, rolling countryside she recognized from travel brochures, the sky as cloudy as all English October skies ought to be, and the ground, of course, unpleasantly damp. She was led into a solitary building done up like an old inn, complete with swinging sign that read THE WHITE STAG, which bore a painted carving of a grayish animal that looked remarkably like a donkey.

Indoors was cozy and hot, both effects produced by an unseasonably large fire. A woman in Regency dress and marriage cap rose from behind a desk and led Jane to a seat beside the hearth.

"Welcome to 1816. I am Mrs. Wattlesbrook. And what shall we call you?"

"Jane Hayes is fine."

Mrs. Wattlesbrook raised her eyebrows. "Is that so? You are certain you still wish to retain your Christian name? Very well, but we mustn't keep our entire name, right? We shall address you as Miss Jane Erstwhile."

Erstwhile? "Uh, okay."

"And how old are you, Miss Erstwhile?"

"Thirty-three."

Mrs. Wattlesbrook leaned on her arm with an air of impatience. "You misunderstand me. How old *are* you?" she asked, raising her eyebrows significantly. "You are aware that at this time a lady of thirty-three would be an affirmed spinster and considered unmarriageable."

"I'd rather not lie about my age," Jane said, then immediately winced. Here she was entering Austenland where she'd pretend the year was 1816 and that actors were her friends and family and potential suitors, and she worried about shaving a few years off her age? Her stomach shrank, and for the first time she feared she might not be able to see this through.

Mrs. Wattlesbrook was watching her shrewdly. Jane gulped a breath. Could she know? Did she have that uncanny Carolyn intuition, did she sense that Jane was here not as an idle vacationer but because she had a nasty obsession? Or did she assume even worse—that Jane was seeking a fantasy in earnest, that she believed she might find him, find love, on this It's a Small World ride?

Jane's mother often told the story of how until Jane was eight years old, when asked what she wanted to be when she grew up, she still answered with conviction, "I want to be a princess." Perhaps because of her mother's pleasant mockery, by her adolescence, Jane had learned to hide her desires for such wonderful impossibilities as becoming a princess, or a supermodel, or Elizabeth Bennet. Bury and hide them until they were so profound and neglected as to somehow be true. Sheesh, she was feeling ready to stretch herself out on a Freudian couch.

No matter. Mock her if you will, but Jane was determined to dig up those weedy issues and toss them out. She *would* enjoy this last trip to fantasyland so utterly that it'd be easy in three weeks to put it all behind her—Austen, men, fantasies, period. But in order for it to work, she had to be Jane, experiencing everything for herself, and so she clung stubbornly to her actual age.

"I could say 'I'm not yet four and thirty' if you prefer." Jane smiled innocently.

"Quite," said Mrs. Wattlesbrook with firm lips, insistent that there was no humor to be had. "For the duration of your stay, there will be one other guest at Pembrook Park—a Miss Charming, who arrived yesterday. When Miss Amelia Heartwright arrives, she will stay at Pembrook Cottage, so you shall see her often as well. I expect all of you ladies to maintain appropriate manners and conversation even when alone. In other words, no gossip, no swapping university prank stories, no *yo*'s and *ho*'s and all that. I am very strict about my observances, hm?"

She seemed to expect a response, so Jane said, "I read your warning in my social history notes."

Mrs. Wattlesbrook raised her eyebrows. "A reader? How refreshing." She made a show of sorting through Jane's papers, humming theatrically, then looked up, half her eyes hidden under the flap of her cap. "I know why you are here."

She knew!

"We receive extensive financial statements, and I know you did not pay your own way, so let us put that drama out of the way, shall we?"

"Is it a drama?" Jane said with a laugh, relieved the woman was just referring to Carolyn's bequest.

"Hm?" Mrs. Wattlesbrook would not budge from her intended course of conversation. Jane sighed.

"Yes, my great-aunt left me this vacation in her will, but I don't know what you mean by *drama*. I never intended to hide—"

"No need to make a fuss." She waved her arms as if wafting Jane's exclamations out the window like a foul odor. "You are here, you are paid in full. I would not have you worry that we will not take care of you just because you are not our usual type of guest and there is no chance, given your economic conditions, that you would ever be a repeat client or likely to associate with and recommend us to potential clients. Let me assure you that we will still do all in our power to make your visit, such as it is, enjoyable."

Mrs. Wattlesbrook smiled, showing both rows of yellowing teeth. Jane blinked. Economic conditions? Usual type of guest? She made herself take two deep-rooted yoga breaths, smiled back, and thought of men in breeches. "Okay then."

"Good, good." Mrs. Wattlesbrook patted Jane's arm, suddenly the picture of hospitality and maternal tenderness. "Now, do have some tea. You must be quite chilled from your journey."

In fact, the temperature of the limo, unlike this pseudo-inn, had been quite comfortable, and in the blazing heat the last thing Jane wanted was hot tea, but she reminded herself to play along, so she sweated and drank.

Mrs. Wattlesbrook settled down to quiz her on the items of study—how to play the card games whist and speculation, general etiquette, current events of the Regency period, and so on. Jane answered like a nervous teenager giving an oral report.

Then off to the wardrobe where she put on a calf-length, nightgownlike chemise and over it tried on a series of push-up bra corsets. This exercise made swimming suit shopping seem like a walk in the park. Eventually they did find one that didn't dig her under the arms but gently encouraged posture and did her the voluptuous justice all Regency breasts demanded.

"I'll just keep these for you until your return," Mrs. Wattlesbrook said, picking up Jane's purple bra and panties at arm's length and handing her an awkward pair of white cotton drawers. To properly enjoy "the Experience," Jane was to understand, even the underwear must be Regency. A lot, apparently, must be sacrificed to fully benefit from the Experience, except makeup. The Rules of Pembrook Park, Jane was realizing, were not overly concerned with creating a true historical setting.

The proprietress opened a wardrobe and revealed that Jane's measurements had been transformed into four day dresses, three evening dresses, a ball gown in white and lace, two short "spencer" jackets, a brown fitted overcoat called a "pelisse," two bonnets, a bright red shawl, and a pile of chemises, drawers, stockings, boots, and slippers.

"Wow. I mean, wow," was all Jane could say for a few moments. She wiggled her fingers like an evil miser at a horde of riches. "They're all for me?"

"For your *use*, yes, though not to keep, mind. Your great-aunt's payment did not cover wardrobe souvenirs." Mrs. Wattlesbrook extracted a dress from Jane's eager fingers and packed it tenderly into her trunk. "This is an evening dress. You should wear a day dress now, the pink one there."

The pink one was hideous. Jane took the blue one off its hook, ignoring Mrs. Wattlesbrook's offended sniff.

In a few minutes, the dressing-of-Jane was complete: blue print day dress trimmed in dark blue ribbon with elbow-length sleeves, stockings fastened to thighs with garters, black ankle boots, and there she was. She stood sideways, looked in the mirror, and experienced a silly, naughty feeling, like she hadn't had since the sinful pleasure of playing Barbie dolls with her younger cousin when she was twelve and should've been too old. Here she was, a grown woman playing dress-up, but it felt so good.

"And there she is," Jane whispered.

"I must have any electronic thingies now, my dear."

Jane turned over her MP3 player.

"And?" Mrs. Wattlesbrook tipped her head up to look at Jane through the spectacles resting on her nose. "Nothing else?" She paused as though waiting for Jane to confess, which she did not. Mrs. Wattlesbrook sighed and removed the player from the room, carrying it between finger and thumb like something dead to be flushed down the toilet. While she was out, Jane hid her cell phone in the bottom of the trunk. She'd already gone to the trouble to set up international service with her provider because it would be unbearable to be without e-mail for three weeks. Besides, it gave her a little glee to sneak something illegal across the border. She wasn't the usual type of client, was she? Then she certainly wouldn't try to act like it.

Jane dined that night with Mrs. Wattlesbrook and practiced manners during the longest two-hour meal she had lived through since attending the eighth annual Researchers for a Better Paper Pulp (RBPP) banquet with boyfriend #9 (keynote address: "The Climax and the Downfall of the Wood Chip").

"When eating fish, use your fork in your right hand and a piece of bread in your left. Just so. No knives with fish or fruit, because the knives are silver and the acids in those foods tarnish. Remember, you must never talk to the servants during dinner. Don't even mention them, don't make eye contact. Think of it as demeaning to them, if you must, but find a way to obey this society's rules, Miss Erstwhile. It is the only way to truly appreciate the Experience. I need not warn you again about behavior with regard to the opposite sex. You are a young, single woman and should never be unchaperoned with a gentleman indoors and only out-of-doors so long as you are in motion—riding, walking, or in a carriage, that is. No touching, besides the necessary social graces, such as taking a man's hand as he helps you down from a carriage or his arm as he escorts you into dinner. No familiar talk, no intimate questions. I am to understand from past clients that when romance blooms under the tension of these restrictions, it is all the more passionate."

After dinner, Mrs. Wattlesbrook led Jane into the main room of the inn, where an older woman in a brown Regency dress waited at the piano.

"As you will have opportunity to attend informal dances and a ball, you must perfect a minuet and two country dances. Theodore, come in here."

A man in perhaps his late twenties came into the inn's main room. Jane caught a glimpse of a worn paperback novel in his hand before he stashed it behind the piano. He wore his hair a little long, though he didn't sport the midjaw sideburns Jane liked so well, and he was, she thought, taller than a man should be if he doesn't play basketball.

"This is Theodore, an under-gardener at the estate, but I've taught him the dances, and he stands in for a gentleman on the first night so our guests can practice."

She put out her hand. "Hi, I'm Jane."

"No, you are not!" Mrs. Wattlesbrook said. "You are Miss

Erstwhile. And you are not to talk to him, he is just a servant. For the sake of the Experience, we must be proper."

Mrs. Wattlesbrook was reminding Jane of Miss April, the spiteful, tight-bunned, glossy-lipped, stick-cracking ballet teacher of her elementary school years. She hadn't much cared for Miss April.

When Mrs. Wattlesbrook turned her back to give instructions to the piano player, Jane mouthed to Theodore, "Sorry."

Theodore smiled, a fantastically broad smile that made her notice just how blue his eyes were.

"The minuet is a ceremonious, graceful dance," said Mrs. Wattlesbrook, closing her eyes to enjoy the music the pianist drew from the keys. "It commences each ball as a means of introducing all the members of the society. Each couple takes turns in the center performing the figures. Curtsy to the audience, Miss Erstwhile, now to your partner, and begin."

With Mrs. Wattlesbrook calling the motions, Jane wove, swerved, minced, and spun. She had thought it might be awkward dancing with a man a foot taller than her, but this was no waltz or high school slow dance. It was a smooth combination of figures, of taking hands and releasing, turning and returning.

Jane found herself giggling when she missed a step or turned the wrong way. It was a bit embarrassing, but she took comfort in the fact that she didn't snort. Her partner smiled, apparently amused by her own amusement. Though at a formal ball they would be wearing gloves, in this informal setting their hands were bare, and she felt the calluses on his palm when he took her hand, felt him get warmer as they danced on. It was strange to touch someone like this, touch hands, feel his hand on her back, on her waist, walking her through the figures, and yet not know him at all. Never even have heard the sound of his voice.

He wrapped his hand around her waist. She blushed like a freshman.

After the minuet they practiced two country dances. The first was spunky, and she had to learn how to "skip elegantly." She had square-danced for a sixth-grade assembly once (a tragic affair involving boyfriend #1), and the second number reminded her of a sedate Virginia reel.

"The top couple moves up and down the center and the rest wait," explained Mrs. Wattlesbrook. "In a ball with many couples, one dance can take half an hour."

"So that's why Elizabeth and Mr. Darcy had time to talk," Jane said, "as they stood there waiting their turn at the top."

"Indeed," said Mrs. Wattlesbrook.

Blunder, Jane thought, glancing at her partner. What must he think of her? A woman who memorized Austen books and played dress-up? She'd enjoyed a bit of flirting as they danced, but she was too embarrassed to meet his eyes again. When they finished, he left the way he'd come in.

Jane sat that night on her hard mattress in the inn's guest room, feeling loose and pretty in her clean white chemise, her arms around her knees. The English countryside was framed by her window as though it were a painting, blue and purple, abstract in the low light. She grimaced as she thought about the dance, re-membering how fun it had been until she'd spoiled it at the end. She didn't want that for this experience. She needed a good end-ing, the best ending, though her imagination couldn't dredge up exactly what that should be.

The endings of all her relationships had displaced any previ-ous loveliness. In memory, the jokes faded, the personalities of the various boyfriends blurred together, weekend trips were truncated in thought to as long as it took her to scratch her neck. The entire relationship was condensed and reformed in her mind to be solely about its ending.

Here she was at the beginning of something, her toes curled

over the edge of the diving board. She was ready to plunge. Good-bye to her awkward list of numbered boyfriends and her mutated, Austen-inspired intensity that had pushed her from one ending to another. She was determined that this vacation, this holiday, unlike any of her relationships, would have a very good ending.

Let's glance back a moment and remember: Jane's First Love

Alex Ripley, AGE FOUR

Alex declared to Jane's preschool teachers, both their parents, and Cindy (the girl with self-cut bangs) that he and Jane would marry. After a rousing Easter egg hunt in the park, he ran with Jane behind a tree.

"I want to give you something that means we'll be together forever."

He kissed her on the lips seven times. It reminded Jane of a chicken pecking. A soft chicken.

That summer Alex's parents moved to Minnesota. She never saw him again.

day 1

THE NEXT MORNING AFTER A huge, meaty breakfast, Jane climbed into a carriage (A carriage! she thought), her trunk fastened to the back. Mrs. Wattlesbrook stood in the doorway, dabbing a handkerchief to her dry eyes.

"Do have a good time, Miss Erstwhile, and remember to wear a wrap and bonnet when you go out!"

The day was gray, and patchy rain nudged the carriage roof. Jane watched the hilly country bounce by, a row of river trees huddling in a line. The fresh landscape encouraged her artist's eye to see in paint colors—leaves of sap green, the distant roofs of a small town in burnt umber and cadmium red, the sky cerulean blue. They passed a gate and guard station, and rolled up an unpaved private drive. The carriage slowed then halted in front of a stately Georgian manor, yellow bricks, white gables, and sixteen facing windows. It looked clean and square and full of something secret and wonderful, a solidly wrapped present.

"That's a fair prospect," Jane breathed, giving herself chills.

The front doors opened and a dozen people filed out. Despite the weather, they stood patiently in two lines, blinking against the thin rainfall. From their attire, Jane guessed they were mostly house servants plus a few gardeners in rougher clothes. Theodore was difficult to miss, a head taller than any other.

The carriage lurched to a stop and gave Jane a sinking feeling in her middle. Now that it came to it, she didn't know if she could role-play with a straight face. She was used to having clothes that touched her waist and her hips, hair loose around her face, pants with a back pocket to keep a few bucks handy, shoes that allowed her to run. She felt so ridiculously phony riding up in a carriage in this Halloween costume, pretending to be someone of note, all those servants and actors knowing she was just a sad woman with odd fantasies. She felt naked and pale in her empire-waist dress.

One of the manservants opened the carriage door and held out his hand. Jane made a muted whine in her throat, then hoped he hadn't heard her.

Okay, okay, I can do this, Jane said to herself. Of course I can do this. I should be used to making a fool out of myself by now.

33

This will be the last big one. Just three weeks and then I can leave this part of myself behind and get on with my life. And maybe it'll be fun. It might even be fun.

She took the servant's hand, stepped down from the carriage, breathed in a steadying breath, and caught an anachronistic whiff of Polo. Somehow that smell was reassuring.

"My dear Jane, you are very welcome!" A woman of perhaps fifty years approached the carriage on the arm of a red-cheeked, chubby man. Her blue dress and red umbrella were bright and inviting against the dreary backdrop of servants and rain.

"I am your aunt Saffronia, though of course you do not remember me as I haven't kissed your cheeks since you were two and your widowed mother married that American and took you off to the New World," she said neatly in one breath. "How we mourned your loss! My, but it is so good of you to come and visit at last. This is my husband, Sir John Templeton. He is near expiring in the anticipation of your arrival."

Sir John blew up his cheeks and chewed on some invisible cud.

"Go on, Sir John, say hello," Aunt Saffronia said.

Sir John at last fixed his wandering gaze on Jane. "Yes, well, hello," he said.

He blinked lazily, and assuming he meant it as a nod of greeting, Jane curtsied as Mrs. Wattlesbrook had taught her.

"Hello, Uncle. How are you?"

"I had some ham for breakfast. I do not get ham much, what with pigs such dirty beasts and not on the property." His gaze wandered.

Jane tried to think of some appropriate response to that. She came up with, "Hooray for ham!"

"Yes, lovely," said Aunt Saffronia. "Lovely, indeed. You are lovely. It has been a long time since we have had lovely young people at Pembrook Park . . ." Her voice trailed off and she lifted a finger-nail to her mouth, then pulled back abruptly. Jane thought it was a small error—the actress bit her nails, but Aunt Saffronia did not.

Sir John cleared his throat with a bit more phlegm involved than made Jane comfortable. "Young people? Lady Templeton, you forget Miss Charming."

"Ah, yes, of course! How could I forget Miss Charming? She is the daughter of a dear friend and only arrived yesterday. What fortunate timing for you, I think. It is so nice for young people to share each other's company."

Aunt Saffronia took Jane's arm and led her upstairs to a comfortable-sized room with a canopied bed, baby blue walls, sparsely furnished, not gothic enough to tempt her to look for "Catherine Heathcliff" engravings on the windowsill. It was ex-actly the kind of room Jane would have imagined. She couldn't think why this discovery was disappointing. It was slightly more disheartening to discover that the "kerosene" lamp by her bed had a flame-shaped lightbulb and was plugged into an outlet.

Jane dismissed her properly taciturn maid, Matilda, saying that she would rest until dinner, since the jet lag was making grav-ity feel alarmingly heavy. She spent a fidgety hour on a soft mat-tress, lifted up the sheets to spy out a DEVON brand tag, then poked around in the attached bathroom and found a flush toilet and bathtub with running water. It was a relief not to have to use a bedpan, but it also made her feel more guilty than ever. The less historical vigor observed, the more difficult it was for Jane to pre-tend that this whole exercise was anything beyond wish fulfill-ment. She felt too weird to rest.

The day continued to drizzle, so she ambled the burgundy corridors, peeking into open doors. The house was perfect. It even carried the old, clean smell of a museum. Her heart pounded a bit, and she felt as if she had sneaked away from a tour guide.

She walked a long gallery with north-facing windows and matched gazes with the portraits. Men and women in stiff costumes, old jewelry, their backgrounds faded countryside, their eyes imperious. They were marvelous. She wondered if those rich people had naturally looked on the world with such assurance of their own nobility or if the painter had created it for them. An itch inside her hand made her want to give it a try, but she scratched the desire away. She hadn't picked up a paintbrush since college.

She ran out of upstairs, so down she went, only to be stopped fast by voices coming from a sitting room. Jane wasn't ready to face real people yet, not as Miss Erstwhile. The portraits had been intimidating enough. Footsteps scared her out of the hall and into an open doorway. It was a large, square, empty room, wooden floors, no furniture. The grand hall. The place where balls happen. The walls were an impatient green, the crystals on the chandeliers winked in the window light. If she were the type of person who looked for signs, Jane would have thought the room was shivering in anticipation of something momentous. But she wasn't.

She turned to leave, and from the far door saw the dark outline of a man enter. He stopped. She stopped. She couldn't see his face.

"Pardon," he said and turned back.

She stood staring at where he'd been for a few moments, relieved at first that she hadn't been forced to make conversation yet, then soon, actually sorry that he'd gone. Just his presence had set her heart to pounding, and the feeling prickled in her the delightful expectation of things to come.

Goody, she thought.

As she ascended the main staircase on the way back to her room, she bumped into a woman bending over her own boots, the curve in her back declaring that she wasn't wearing a corset.

"Dratted drawers," said the woman, straightening.

She was unnaturally buxom, in her fifties, and sported short, bleached hair heavily sprayed and an attached fake bun of a slightly different shade. Her eyes widened when she saw Jane, and her surgery-tightened skin stretched to admit a wide smile.

"Well, hello, you're new, aren't you? My name's Miss Elizabeth Charming, like Elizabeth Bennet, see? But don't you like the last name? It was Mrs. Wattlesbrook's idea. I'd thought just to go ahead and name myself Elizabeth Bennet, because I mean to bag a Mr. Darcy, but she thought Elizabeth Charming was more enchanting. Anyhoo, my friends call me Eliza." She stuck out her left hand, the ring finger of which still bore the mark of a recently removed wedding band. Jane shook it awkwardly with her right hand, then bobbed a curtsy.

"Hello, I suppose I'm Jane Erstwhile."

"You're one of those Americans."

Jane frowned, confused. Clearly this woman was also from the United States, possibly from a southern state—the accent was unclear. Then Jane realized that she was attempting to sound British, over-pronouncing words and occasionally dropping an "r." The effect made her sound like a little girl in desperate need of a speech therapist.

"Oh dear," Eliza said miserably. "I don't think I'm supposed to talk to you until we've been properly introduced. Let's pretend we haven't met."

Eliza started back down the stairs, stuffing one breast more snugly into her dress, then turned back again to speak low and urgently into Jane's ear. "And by the way, I'm twenty-two. I told Mrs. Wattlesbrook and now I'm telling you. I didn't forgo a new car and a month in Florence to be fifty again." She patted Jane's behind and trudged down the stairs, holding her long skirts above her ankles.

* * *

THAT EVENING, THEY WERE FORMALLY introduced.

"Jane, my dear, you do look lovely!" Aunt Saffronia said.

Jane nearly blushed as she descended the stairs. She did feel lovely, actually, if a little too aware of her own breasts exposed within the lower neck of the evening dress. Her maid, Matilda, had helped her with her hair, attaching a bunch of curls (she flattered herself that they looked more natural than Miss Charming's bundle of plastic) and winding pretty little beads around her head. She had been wary of empire waists, but the feel of the fabric and the splendid rust and yellow of her evening dress made her feel so different that she girded herself up to start the make-believe.

You can do it, you can do it, she chanted silently as if she were attempting the last set in kickboxing. She hated kickboxing.

"Jane, may I introduce our house guest Miss Elizabeth Charming of Hertfordshire?"

"How do you do, Miss Erstwhile, what-what?" said Miss Charming, her tightened lips trembling with the effort of approximating a British accent. "Spit spot I hope, rather."

"How do you do?"

They both curtsied and Miss Charming made a silent "shh" with her lips, as though Jane would out her for the stairway meeting. Jane had a burst of maternal instinct that made her want to cuddle Miss Charming and help her through this crazy Austenland maze. If she only knew the way herself.

"Miss Charming is about your age, I believe," Aunt Saffronia said.

"Oh no, Aunt, I'm quite certain that Miss Charming, still in the bloom of her youth, is several years my junior."

Miss Charming giggled. Aunt Saffronia smiled graciously as she took Jane's arm, and the three walked into the drawing room. At their entrance, two gentlemen stood.

Ah, the gentlemen.

They wore the high-collared vests, cravats, buttoned coats with long tails, and tight little breeches that had driven Jane's imagination mad on many an uneventful Tuesday night. Her heart bumped around in her chest like a bee at a window, and everything seemed to move in closer, the world pressing against her, insisting that all was real and there for the touching. She was really here. Jane held her hands behind her back in case they trembled with eagerness.

"Jane, may I present Colonel Andrews, Sir John's cousin and the second son of the earl of Denton? He passed the partridge-shooting season with us and we have been fortunate enough to persuade him to stay on for the pheasant season. Colonel Andrews, my niece from America, Miss Jane Erstwhile."

Colonel Andrews was fair-haired with a decent set of shoulders and a very ready smile. He could not seem more pleased to see her, bowing without removing his gaze from her face.

"What a pleasure, a very pleasant pleasure, indeed." The way his tone slid over his words gave him a delightful, roguish appeal that made Jane want to kiss him on the spot. Or the lips, whichever was closer.

Hm, maybe she really could see this through.

"And this is his good friend Mr. Nobley," Aunt Saffronia said, "who has agreed to honor us with his presence for some of the hunting season while his estate is under renovation."

Mr. Nobley was taller than Colonel Andrews, and his jaw was in no need of the long sideburns to give it definition. The line of his shoulders identified him as the most likely of the bunch to have been the shadowy lurker from the great hall. In the light, she found him handsome, in a brooding sort of way.

Of course, Jane thought, one man of each type for the buffet. Don't mind if I do.

Mr. Nobley bowed stiffly, then walked away to look out the window.

"How do you do?" said Jane to his back.

Aunt Saffronia laughed. "Do not mind Mr. Nobley. He is annoyed to be trapped here with such minor country gentry, are you not, sir?"

Mr. Nobley looked back at Aunt Saffronia. "I do not know what you mean, madam." His eyes flicked to Jane.

She found herself thinking, I wonder if he thinks I'm pretty? Then thought, don't be silly, it's all an act. Then thought, What fun!

"And you gentlemen already have made the acquaintance of Miss Charming."

"Indeed," said Colonel Andrews, bowing again.

"You boys know you can call me Lizzy."

Jane glanced at Aunt Saffronia, wondering what would happen to this request. According to the Rules, it was completely improper for a man to call a woman by her first name unless they were engaged. Before Aunt Saffronia could speak or Mrs. Wattlesbrook magically appear with a disapproving look, Colonel Andrews came to the rescue.

"I would never dream of doing you such a dishonor, Miss Charming." His voice drew out all the allure in her name, and he smiled with a sly, teasing expression.

Miss Charming giggled. "Tallyho."

Oh no, thought Jane as she watched the exchange, panic tickling her heart. Oh no, oh no, they'll assume I'm a Miss Charming. I don't want to be a Miss Charming!

She tried to catch Mr. Nobley's eye and somehow smile or wink or do anything to indicate that she would never say "tally-ho." He didn't look away from the window, and after a few moments, Jane had cause to be relieved. In a burst of panic, she had actually been ready to *wink* at him. Yikes.

The dinner bell rang. Sir John, who had been slouching in a

chair, roused at the sound and offered his arm to Miss Charming. He patted her hand and grumbled in a too-loud voice, "Let us hope there are enough game birds tonight. My stomach is not up to much boiled mutton, what."

Aunt Saffronia took Mr. Nobley's arm, leaving Jane and the colonel at the tail end of the parade from drawing room to dining room. The precedence told Jane two things: Mr. Nobley must be very rich and well connected to outrank an earl's second son, and she was the lowest-ranking woman. She supposed that was no surprise, considering she was not their "usual type of guest."

They ate pigeon soup with lemons and asparagus, then heaped their own plates in self-service Regency style with fish and grouse, cooked celery and cucumbers. A cup of something like creamy applesauce served as dessert, and the wine was exchanged for Madeira. The food was pretty good, though a bit bland. When would Indian food arrive in England to spice things up? Jane thought she could go for a decent curry.

Aunt Saffronia kept the conversation flowing about the weather, the state of pheasants in the park this year, and the doings of mythic acquaintances in the city. Jane did not speak much during dinner, still oppressed with jet lag and curious to observe before opening her mouth and proving herself a fool. Mr. Nobley, too, barely spoke. Not that Miss Charming at his side didn't do her best.

"What do you think of *me dress*, Mr. Nobley?"

"It is very nice."

"Do you like the fish?"

"Yes, it is a good fish."

"Do I have something in my eye?" This spoken while twisting toward him, her amazing bosom pressing against his shoulder.

No way Mrs. Wattlesbrook could find a corset to fit that, Jane thought.

"I . . . I am afraid I cannot see well in this low light," Mr. Nobley said without really looking.

Miss Charming giggled. "You're quite a bloke, Mr. Nobley. Rather!"

After dinner, the ladies retired to the drawing room while the men stayed in the dining room to pass around snuff and port, which activities the Rules forbade them from doing in front of women. Aunt Saffronia sat between one real and one electric kerosene lamp, embroidering and chattering about the gentlemen, while Miss Charming paced the drawing room floor.

"The colonel is all kindness, is he not, Miss Charming? He has such a sad reputation in the city, I have heard, for carousing and card playing and the like, but I say, what else is a young, unattached man to do with the war over, thanks be, and he the younger son with no title to claim him? A small mercy his mother is not alive to see how he's turned out, rest her. Now Mr. Nobley, of course, is most respectable, perhaps too respectable, what do you say, Jane? No title, but an old, solid family name and wonderful lands. He will be a steadying influence on the colonel, a solid oar for a dinghy. He has such high connections and such a dignified bearing, though I tease him that he seems a bit stiff—"

"Do they really have to drink port alone?" Miss Charming asked, pacing at double speed. "Can't they come any faster?"

"Ah, here they are," Aunt Saffronia said.

Jane smelled a mild waft of alcohol and tobacco sweep before them, and the gentlemen emerged triumphant—shiny colonel, glowering gentleman, soggy husband.

Aunt Saffronia proposed a rousing game of whist to pass the evening. Miss Charming, seemingly bored of trying to seduce the Darcy out of Mr. Nobley, secured Colonel Andrews as a partner. Jane played opposite Aunt Saffronia. As for the rest of the party, Sir John drank from a crystal decanter (probably full of cherry

Kool-Aid, Jane guessed), while Mr. Nobley read a book and generally ignored everybody.

Jane focused on the rules of whist, losing horribly. She felt
like hand-washed laundry, rubbed and heavy and ready to be laid
out to dry. Her routine-addicted brain never handled time changes
well, and the cards and conversation and exhaustion melted together, making her dizzy. She looked up to ground herself in her
surroundings.

Mr. Nobley was absorbed in his book. She looked left. Colonel Andrews was grinning at her, his smile conscious of just how
smoking hot he really was. All around her were yellow walls, gaudy
Georgian finery, the deliciously historic smell of furniture wax
and kerosene. She looked down at herself, dressed in foreign fabric, cleavage encased in rust-colored satin, slippered feet resting
on an Oriental rug. She was completely ridiculous. At the same
time, she wanted to stomp the ground and squeal like a teenager
just asked to prom. She was here!

And if this were an Austen novel, the characters would be up
for a little banter about now. Jane cleared her throat.

"Mr. Nobley, Lady Templeton says Pembrook Park will host
a ball in just over a fortnight. Do you enjoy a good dance?"

"Dancing I tolerate," he answered in a dry tone. "I might say
I enjoy a *good* dance, though I have never had one."

"Scandalous!" Aunt Saffronia said. "You have danced in this
drawing room several times, and I have seen you escort many a
fine young lady onto a ballroom floor. Are you saying that none of
those qualified as a good dance?"

"Madam, you may choose to understand my comments any
way you like."

Jane glared. He was, in his subtle manner, insulting dear Aunt
Saffronia! Wait, no he wasn't, they were both actors playing parts.
Being inside this story felt a tad more surreal than she'd expected.

For one thing, if this were real, she'd find Mr. Nobley's arrogance annoying and his self-absorption unbearably boring. The character deserved a good thrashing.

"I suppose the lack in all such occurrences was to be found in your partners, Mr. Nobley?" Jane asked.

Mr. Nobley thought. "In them, yes, and partly in myself. I cannot imagine a dance truly being enjoyable unless both partners find themselves equals in rank, grace, and aptitude, as well as naturally fond of each other."

"One might say the same for conversation."

"Indeed one might," he said, turning in his chair to face her. "We are ill-fated in that our society demands we engage in unworthy conversations and dances in order to seem courteous, and yet such actions are ultimately vulgar."

"But pray tell, Mr. Nobley," Jane said, enthused, "how is one to find out if another is her equal in rank, grace, and aptitude, and how is one to discover a natural fondness, without first engaging in conversations and social gatherings? Would you say a hunter were vulgar when coursing through the fields and only dignified when actually shooting at prey?"

"I think she has you there, Nobley," Colonel Andrews said with a laugh.

Mr. Nobley's expression did not change. "A hunter need not spend hours with a pheasant to know it would make a good dinner. A pheasant is nothing more than what it seems, as are hens, foxes, and swans. People are no different. Some may need endless hours of prattle and prancing to know another's worth. I should not."

Jane turned her gaping mouth into a smile. "So, you can tell the worth, the merit, the nobility of a person at a glance?"

"And you cannot?" His expression held a mild challenge. "Can you tell me that within the first few moments of knowing each person in this room, you had not formed firm judgments of their character, which up to this very moment you have not questioned?"

She smiled ever so slightly. "You are correct, sir. However, I do hope that, in at least one regard, my first impression will eventually prove not to be *completely* accurate."

There was a tense silence, and then Colonel Andrews laughed again.

"Excellent. Most excellent. Never heard someone give old Nobley the what-for quite like that." He slapped the table emphatically.

"Come on, Miss Erstwhile," Miss Charming said, "it's your turn, what-what."

Jane played her card, and after a moment stole a glance at Mr. Nobley. He'd been watching her, and when he looked away, guilt betrayed his forced serenity. Sir John, a nearly empty glass trembling in his hand, snorted in his sleep on the sofa. Jane heard Miss Charming say "jolly good" again, caught Colonel Andrews passing her a sly smile, and found herself wondering if she wasn't the prettiest, smartest guest they'd had in some time. Or ever.

All was going splendidly.

And here we begin with Jane's ill-fated, numbered list of boyfriends.
Boyfriend #1

Justin Kimble, AGE TWELVE

According to sixth-grade reckoning, Jane and Justin had been "going out" since fourth grade, when he'd shared his Pixy Stix with her during the class carnival. This meant that Justin sometimes pushed her in the hall, Jane gave him significant valentines (I "heart" you), and whenever receiving a "rating phone call" asking them to score classmates on looks and personality, both scored the other as a ten.

Then came the fateful day Mrs. Davis went through her class list, letting each boy pick his folk dance partner for the upcoming "Hooray for Culture!" assembly.

Mrs. Davis called Justin's name.

Jane sat up.

Justin said, "Hattie Spinwell."

Hattie flipped her hair.

For years after, there were few things Jane distrusted so much as the words "guy's choice."

THE NEXT MORNING THEY EXPECTED a visit from the guest of Pembrook Cottage, but the rain was so dense, Jane felt as trapped as if the estate were surrounded by a moat. At least the wet kept the gentlemen from hunting.

"You will simply adore Amelia Heartwright," Aunt Saffronia said as the ladies embroidered in the sitting room. Jane eyed her aunt's neat little flowers and fields of cross-stitches. She was transforming her own fruit basket sampler into a knotted mass that resembled a cornucopia beaten and left for dead. Miss Charming had abandoned her embroidery in favor of pacing by the door, ready for the first sign of the gentlemen's return from billiards.

"She has been living in the city this past year and is only just returning to the country to tend to her mother in her declining health. Her mother, Mrs. Heartwright, is Sir John's widow aunt. It is so good of him to give her the cottage. I have not seen Amelia Heartwright in a year at least. Last she was here—" Aunt Saffronia glanced at the hallway and then at the window as if suspecting eavesdroppers. She lowered her voice. "Last she was here, I detected some attachment between her and a young sailor, a certain George East, of decent breeding but no real prospects. I do not know what became of them. Miss Heartwright returned to the city and Mr. East to the sea, I suppose. A shame, even if he was as poor as a farmer. They did seem very fond of each other, but young hearts are fickle things, are they not, Miss Charming?"

"What?" Miss Charming stopped pacing. "I mean, what-what? Just so."

The gentlemen, much to Miss Charming's palpable elation, did conclude their billiards and join the ladies for tiffin and tea, charades and gossip. Jane sat beside Colonel Andrews. He had a dashing smile. It nearly dashed right off his face.

Another day, another night followed of pleasant meals, conversations indoors, restful afternoons watching the rain thicken the panes. No great events transpired, and Jane found that to be a relief. She still felt dried up and brittle in this new pretend skin, and she really didn't think she could stomach false declarations of love and bogus trysts. Yet. Eighteen more days to go. There would be time to celebrate her last hurrah, to face Mr. Darcy and say good-bye forever. So for now, she relaxed. She couldn't remember the last time she'd had the luxury of taking an afternoon nap. It felt scandalous.

But when the rain lifted on her third day, her muscles awoke and scolded her for so much sitting. It had been nearly a week since she had last done anything that in good conscience could be considered "exercise." She wasn't a health nut (those people could be so irritating), she was just a touch obsessive-compulsive, thank you very much, and if she didn't follow her compulsion to exercise hard, her body freaked out on her and began to demand she eat enough sugar to choke her pancreas. She had wandered the grand house and found no hidden gym (Mrs. Wattlesbrook's Ideal Client, apparently, insisted on mascara but not a StairMaster), so Jane excused herself after the sausage and jellied-egg breakfast, saying she desired a solitary walk around the gardens. She was wearing her least favorite day dress (the pink one with little rosebuds that resembled splattered tomato sauce) and so felt no fear for its ruin when, once out of sight of the house windows, she held the hem above her knees and ran.

It was awkward in her ankle boots, the slap-slap of her uncushioned feet soon insisting she tone it down to a speed walk. Even so, speed-walking in a corset was surprisingly vigorous, and soon the cool autumn day began to feel like a crispy hot Texas summer. She was sitting on a bench, her skirts bunched up on her thighs and her elbows resting on her knees as she tried to slow her breathing, when she heard a male voice.

"Um, I think I should tell you I'm here."

Jane sat upright, quickly pulling her skirts back down to her ankles. She had been wearing drawers, of course, but it still felt absurdly immodest to sit that way in 1816 attire. She looked around, seeing no one.

"Where are you?" she asked.

Theodore, her dance partner of late, stood from behind the bush directly in front of her. His impressive height made it seem that he was slowly expanding while standing up, like stretched taffy.

"What were you doing back there?"

"I'm a gardener," he said, raising the shovel and pick like a show of evidence. "I was just working here, I wasn't trying to spy."

"You, uh, caught me there at an unladylike moment. Mrs. Wattlesbrook would probably box my ears."

"That's why I spoke. I wanted to let you know you were not alone before you did something—something worse."

"Like what?"

"Whatever women do when they think they're alone." He laughed. "I don't know. I don't know what I'm talking about, you surprised me and I'm just—" His smile dropped. "Sorry, I shouldn't talk . . . I'm not supposed to talk to you."

"Well, you already have. We may as well meet for real this time, without old Wattlesbrook spying. I'm Jane."

"Theodore the gardener," he said, wiping off his hand and then offering it to her. She shook it, wondered if they should be bowing and curtsying, but is that what you do with a gardener? The entire conversation felt forbidden, like a secret Austen chapter that she discovered longhand in some forgotten file.

"The gardens look lovely."

"Thank you, ma'am."

Ma'am? she thought.

"So," he said, his eyes taking in everything but her face, "you're from the former colonies?"

She looked hard at him to detect if he was serious. He glanced at her, then down again, and sort of bowed. She laughed.

He tossed his pick into the ground. "I can't play this. I sound completely daft."

"Why would you have to *play* anything?"

"I'm supposed to be invisible. You don't know all the lectures we heard on the matter—stay out of the way, look down, don't bother the guests. I shouldn't have said a word, but I was afraid of getting stuck behind that shrub all day trying not to make a peep. Or worse, you discovering me after a time and thinking I was a lecherous lunatic trying to peek up your skirt. So, anyhow, how do you do, the name's Martin Jasper, originally from Bristol, raised in Sheffield, enjoy seventies rock and walks in the rain, and please don't tell Mrs. Wattlesbrook. I need this job."

"I didn't exactly find Mrs. Wattlesbrook the kind of lady I'd be tempted to confide in. Don't worry, Martin."

"Thanks. Guess I should leave you to your lady stuff." He picked up his tools and walked away.

Jane stared after him, certain he was a bit loony, if handsomely so. Then again, perhaps many wealthy and elderly twenty-year-old women had ratted on forward servants in the past. He likely had the right to be paranoid. She just wished he'd known that she was different. Speaking to a real person had been like drinking a cold glass of water after too much sugary punch.

Jane was hurrying back toward the house and the hopes of a bath before the promised call from Pembrook Cottage that afternoon. She turned a bend and knocked right into Mr. Nobley and Colonel Andrews coming from the other direction.

"Excuse me!" she said, backing away. She was afraid she smelled like sweat after her surreptitious speed walk, but perhaps the exercise had also reddened her cheeks and brightened her eyes. One can hope.

"Pardon indeed," said the colonel. "I was just telling Nobley here, I think that divine Miss Erstwhile sneaked off into the grounds alone. Let's see if we cannot find her out."

"Oh." Jane felt herself sway. That encounter with a real person had roused her up inside more than she'd realized. Her dress hung on her shoulders like a potato sack, her bonnet felt like a vise, the sunlight scratched at her skin.

"I don't think I can do this," she whispered, too low for anyone to hear.

"I say, Miss Erstwhile, you are tongue-tied today," Colonel Andrews said. "What secrets is your mouth trying to hold back? I must know!"

"Stop it, Andrews," Mr. Nobley said, coming up beside her to take her arm. "Can't you see that she is unwell? Go fetch some water."

The colonel's face was suddenly serious. "Apologies, Miss Erstwhile. Do sit down. I will return swiftly." He set off at once toward the house.

Mr. Nobley put an arm behind her back, guiding her to a nearby boulder, helping her to sit as though she would break if breathed upon. No matter how she protested, he would not let her go.

"If you permit me," he said, crouching beside her, "I will carry you inside."

She laughed. "Wow, that sounds like fun, but really I'm fine.

I don't feel sick, I just feel like a schmuck, and that's not a malady you can throw water at."

"You are homesick?"

Jane sighed, wishing for Molly, but all she had was this strange, sideburned man who was generally as boring as gray and dull as oatmeal. But at least he was listening. She leaned forward, whispering, in case Mrs. Wattlesbrook installed microphones in the shrubbery. "I don't know if I can do this." She shook the skirt of her dress. "I don't know if I can pretend."

He stared at her, unblinking, for long enough to make Jane uncomfortable.

"You are being serious," he said at last. "Miss Erstwhile, why are you here?"

"You'd laugh at me if I told you," she whispered. "No, wait, you wouldn't, it's not in your character."

He blinked as though she'd flicked water at his face.

"Did that sound rude? I didn't mean to. Ugh, I feel so tired. I just want to lie down and sleep until I'm myself again, but I've only been half myself lately, and I thought coming here would let me work this part out of me so I could be me again. I just said 'me' a lot, didn't I?"

He smiled briefly. She noticed that his eyes were dark, a warm brown, and noticing made him a fraction more real to her, not so much set dressing but a person she could actually know.

"Tell me, Mr. Nobley, or whoever you are, how do you do it? How do you pretend?"

Her question seemed to stagger him so profoundly, he held his breath. It surprised Jane that she would notice his breath at all, then she realized how close their faces were, how far she had leaned in to whisper.

"Miss Erstwhile," he said flatly, not moving, "play your little charade, but do not try to trap me. I will not sing for you."

He stood up, glaring, until he turned his back to her and took three steps away.

She sat still on the rock, her insides buzzing like a beehive shaken and tossed away. She almost apologized, but then stopped herself.

Apologize for what? she thought. He's a mean, unpleasant, loathsome man. There's no Darcy in him. And I don't need him to get me through this. I can do this; I want to do this.

She prickled with anger at that jacketed back, and the fury helped her burn away her flimsiness. She looked down and breathed.

Be the dress, she told herself. Be the bonnet, Jane. Stage fright, that's all this is. I'm just afraid of looking like a fool. So stop it. Admit that you are a fool already and do this so you can let it go.

She smoothed the stomach of her dress. She closed her eyes and tried to catch the feel of Austen dialogue—it was like trying to hum one song while listening to another. When she opened her eyes again, Colonel Andrews was sprinting across the lawn, a cup of water sloshing over his hand.

"I have it! I have the water! Never fear." He bowed as he gave it to her, smiling the smile of a rake. She took it and drank. The water tasted of minerals and was deep-earth cold, as though it had been drawn from a well. It hummed in her belly. She could do this.

"Well, gentlemen." She took a breath and smiled at the colonel. "Now that you've found me and watered me, what will you do with me?"

"What a marvelous question! How shall I answer?" Colonel Andrews chuckled low in his throat, mischievous. "No, I will be a good boy. So, what adventure were you on before we bumped into you? Keeping a tryst with a clandestine lover or following a map to hidden treasure?"

"I'll never tell," she said.

Nobley's face was impassive, and when he spoke, his voice was traced with formal boredom. "It was my intent to go riding and leave you be, if you wished so much to walk alone."

"But I will not have it," Colonel Andrews said. "After all that rain, it is far too mucky to go hunting, and I need amusement, so you must go riding with us now that we have caught you. You are my butterfly and I refuse to turn you loose."

She took the colonel's arm as they walked to the stables, turning toward his bewitchingly smooth voice. He asked Jane question after question, hanging on her answers and utterly absorbed in her conversation as though she were a novel he could not bear to put down, his interest pulling her back into character as Miss Erstwhile.

Mr. Nobley walked beside her, then rode beside her, and never said another word. She tried to enjoy riding her pathetically docile mount, but Mr. Nobley's silence felt like a slap. Hadn't he seemed human for a moment, before he got all nasty and turned his back? Hadn't the fake world tumbled away? No, it was a mistake, her own dratted hopefulness building castles again where there was only mud. She'd been wrong to try to lower the Regency curtain with that man. He was an actor. She wouldn't make that mistake again.

Of course, she returned Mr. Nobley's silent treatment. Something about the way he looked at her made her feel naked—not naked-sexy, but naked-embarrassed, naked-he-sees-through-my-idiocy-and-knows-what-a-silly-woman-I-am. And she was still straddling the real world and Austenland too precariously to meet his eyes again that day.

The colonel made her laugh and forget, and so despite feeling slightly sticky and foolish and wrapped in a potato sack, Jane had a pretty nice afternoon. She did keep looking out for the tall gardener, hoping he wouldn't see her pretending to be a lady with two costumed gentlemen. Then once, for a moment, hoping that he would.

JANE DID GET HER BATH and felt the sexier for it, empire waist and all. So, clean and sexy, and fiercely clutching her fake Austenland self, she waited that afternoon in the drawing room for the much-anticipated visit from the denizen of Pembrook Cottage. Jane was wearing one of those small, sheer scarves around her shoulders and knotted at her chest, properly acknowledging that Regency breasts should be veiled during daylight hours. Miss Charming's lacy neck scarf barely covered the recesses of her cleavage, daunted as it was by the tundra expanse of the woman's chest.

Miss Charming was fanning her neck with a hand. Jane did the same. Her dress was of light muslin, but beneath lay chemise, corset, and stockings gartered to her thighs, and the autumn sun was vigorous that day, pounding through the windows and flooding the room. Jane waited faintheartedly for the sound of air-conditioning clicking on. No such luck.

At the sound of the bell, Jane and Miss Charming rose from the sofas, straightened their skirts, and listened for the maid to admit the visitors. The men were elsewhere, of course. Aunt Saffronia was waiting in the hall.

"I know what you're thinking," Miss Charming said with no trace of her faux British accent.

"I'd be very impressed if you did." Just at that moment, Jane had been fantasizing about chocolate soup, a dessert she'd once inhaled at a spiffy restaurant in Florida. There was no chocolate in Pembrook Park, though Jane couldn't figure if that lack was helping or impeding her attempt at make-believe.

"You're hoping that Amelia Heartwright is an old, unattractive thing and that the boys won't like her at all. Am I right?" Miss Charming bobbed on her toes.

"Actually, now that you mention it . . ." Miss Charming made an excellent point. Jane gave her a sheepish smile.

They were both disappointed.

"Girls! Look who is here at last. Miss Amelia Heartwright. Miss Heartwright, may I present Miss Elizabeth Charming and my niece, Miss Jane Erstwhile."

The three ladies curtsied and bowed their heads, and Jane noticed how natural and elegant Miss Heartwright's curtsy seemed. She had clearly been here before and come back for more, one of Mrs. Wattlesbrook's ideal clients. She would know the system, the players, the language and customs. She would be a formidable foe.

And she was lovely. Her (natural-looking) blond hair was long, twisted up with plenty of curls around her face. She had an open, honest face (heart-shaped even, as those old writers might have said), pink cheeks and lips, and darling blue eyes. She was slender and tall and not a day over thirty-nine. Forty-three, tops.

Jane scratched her ankle with a toe beneath her skirt. Miss Charming scowled.

"Mama sends her regrets, Lady Templeton, but she is quite fatigued today," Miss Heartwright said in an infuriatingly real British accent. "She bade me bring these apples from our tree."

Aunt Saffronia took the basket. "Lovely! I will give them to the chef and we shall see what splendid treat he can make out of them. You must stay for dinner, Amelia. I insist."

"Thank you, I will."

Jane and Miss Charming exchanged frowns.

The four ladies sat and chatted, or mostly Miss Heartwright and Aunt Saffronia chatted while Jane and her unhappy ally listened, glumly plucking at their embroidery. But among her other qualities, Miss Heartwright was also generous in her attentions.

"Miss Erstwhile, do you enjoy novels?"

"I do, yes."

"I know they are naughty things, but I devour novels. *The Castle of Otronto* had me in chills."

"Yes, how can I forget that giant helmet?" Jane had done her homework on gothic romances a few years ago, thank goodness, in an attempt to appreciate *Northanger Abbey*. "But Mrs. Radcliffe's writings are my favorite, particularly *The Mysteries of Udolpho*."

Miss Heartwright clapped her hands with delight. "Wonderful! We'll have so much to talk about. I hope you will call on the cottage often during your stay."

Jane was spared an answer when the maid announced that the gentlemen had returned from the fields.

"Show them in, thank you," Aunt Saffronia said.

The gentlemen entered, looking smart in their sporting attire, rough and handsome in grays and browns, redolent of grass and animals. Jane stood before them, thinking about whether an 1816 woman would arise for men, and then fumbled her embroidery, sending it to the ground. Colonel Andrews bent to pick it up. On his breath she caught a whiff of tobacco, which only slightly damaged the pleasing effect of his charming smile up close.

The gentlemen remembered Miss Heartwright from last year, of course, and there was a cordial reunion. Cordial? Jane admitted that they both seemed *awfully* pleased to see her. Well, the colonel was effulgent and Mr. Nobley was polite—but wasn't there a knowing look that passed between them? Did they, the enchanting Miss Heartwright and cold Mr. Nobley, have a *history*?

"You are looking well, Mr. Nobley," Miss Heartwright was saying. Jane nearly gasped. Who said such things to that man? "I hope your arm is quite recovered from the accident last year."

And Mr. Nobley nearly smiled! His eyes did anyway. "You remembered. One of my less graceful moments."

Colonel Andrews guffawed. "I had forgotten!" He turned to Jane. "Nobley here was trying to show off on the ballroom floor—for some lady, no doubt—and he slipped during the minuet and broke his arm! Or was it a sprain?"

"Not a break," Mr. Nobley said.

"Do not be so hasty to spoil it, Nobley. A broken bone makes the better story."

"Indeed you are right, Colonel Andrews," Miss Heartwright said. "And I am near expiring, Mr. Nobley, to see what charming bit of fun you will come up with this time. You must, of course, outdo yourself, or what will we have to talk about next year?"

He bowed, polite but by no means offended. "I am your willing servant and shall have no other object than to seek your amusement."

"Well, that is neatly settled then." Aunt Saffronia was all grin. "What a breath of fresh air you are, Miss Heartwright! You must visit the house every day, as often as you like."

Jane glanced at Miss Charming, who in the past half hour had withered like a carrot forgotten in the back of the refrigerator. She was hunched in the sofa, glaring at her embroidery, twisting her foot around, around, around.

Boyfriend #2

Rudy Tiev, AGE FIFTEEN

Rudy was hil-ar-i-ous and so fine. Wherever he went in school, crowds scooped back, forming into spontaneous audiences, waiting with ready smiles for his wit. Or maybe, Jane considered later, drawing back out of fear?

After four months of school dances, mall movies, and after-homework phone calls with Jane, Rudy's repertoire began to suffer for lack of a fresh subject. Without warning, the heat of his humor veered toward her.

"We were making out, and suddenly she licks my mouth like a cat!" he told a group lunching on the lawn. "Lapped me up like milk. Meow, little pussycat."

In the dizzying weeks that followed, Jane read Pride and Prejudice *for the first time.*

At her ten-year high school reunion, three people remembered Jane as "tiger tongue." Good old Rudy was there, sporting an impressive potbelly and spouting jokes that just couldn't bring in the laughs.

day 4, continued

THAT EVENING (TO MAKE HERSELF feel better after the embarrassing breakdown, not to mention the Heartwright intrusion), Jane donned her favorite evening gown, pale peach with a flattering V-neck and cap sleeves. These last three days, she had been seesawing between giddy headlong rush into fantasyland and existential terror, but sometimes when she slipped into a new dress, the only word that really applied was *huzzah*.

The addition of a fourth woman threw a wrench in the precedence. Aunt Saffronia declared she would dine upstairs, and then it was Jane's turn to say that was nonsense and that she would simply walk from the drawing room to the dining room unescorted. At the back of the line. Like an unwanted puppy. Well, she didn't actually say the part about the puppy. She did enter alone, behind Miss Heartwright and Colonel Andrews, but she told herself she did it with style.

When the gentlemen joined the ladies in the drawing room, Miss Charming was quick on the draw—"I'll pout all evening if you don't, Mr. Nobley, and I'm a very effective pouter"—and secured both the single gentlemen at the whist table. Quite a coup. Miss Heartwright, as the guest that day, naturally made up the fourth.

Jane tried to amuse herself by starting a new embroidery sampler, though the product itself was soon much more amusing than the occupation. Sir John, usually too engaged with his drink to do more than grumble to himself, was particularly attentive to Jane. He stared at her until she was forced to acknowledge him and then topple into his staccato conversation.

"Do you shoot much? Mm? Birds? Miss Erstwhile?"

"Uh, no, I don't hunt."

"Yes, of course. Quite, quite."

"So, uh, do you shoot much?"

"Shoot what?"

"Birds?"

"Birds? Are you chirping about birds? Miss Erstwhile?"

Aunt Saffronia wasn't as quick as usual in detecting uncomfortable situations. She sat by a lamp, an open book on her lap and a glazed expression in her eyes. It made Jane wonder how many breaks the poor woman got. The men were often off doing man things, but Aunt Saffronia always had to be *on*.

"Aunt Saffronia." Jane sat beside her so the others wouldn't hear. "Can I persuade you to retire early? You do so much for all of us, all day long. I don't think anyone would deny you a little rest."

Aunt Saffronia smiled and patted her cheek. "I think I may, just this once. If you promise not to tell."

It was gratifying to see the woman go get some me-time, but of course it meant Jane was left alone on the sofa with Sir John and the sloshing noise of his cud. She sat straight in her corset, shut her eyes, and tried to drown out the sticky sound by concentrating on the voices in conversation at the card table.

Miss Charming: "Crikey, Mr. Nobley, but that was a barmy play!"

Mr. Nobley: "I beg apology, Miss Charming."

Miss Charming: "Apology? Don't you know that means it was good? Right smashing?"

Mr. Nobley: "As you say."

Colonel Andrews: "You must take care with Miss Charming, Nobley. She is a sharp one. I wager she could teach you all sorts of things."

Miss Charming (giggling): "Why, Colonel Andrews, whatever do you mean?"

And whenever the speed of conversation slowed a tad, Miss Heartwright was there to buoy it back up.

"Oh, good play, colonel! I didn't see that one. Well done, Mr. Nobley. You have a fine hand, I wager. Valiantly played, Miss Charming, and what lovely skin you possess."

Miss Heartwright wasn't just nice. Oh no. She was astonishingly engaging. Even Mr. Nobley seemed more responsive than normal. He still hadn't spoken with Jane since she broke character, and she watched him now, wondering if he'd tell Mrs. Wattlesbrook how her break muddied up the Experience. He glanced at her once or twice. That was all.

Meanwhile, Miss Heartwright continued to effuse.

The room had begun to seem unnaturally crowded, the lamps too bright but the light they made too dim. Jane caught a glimpse of herself in a mirror, propped up in that ridiculous dress, gawky and silly, a clump of brown bun and curls pinned to her head. Just the sight was enough to tip her back again.

"What a crackpot," she whispered to herself. In all the years Jane had fantasized about an Austenland, she never considered how, once inside its borders, she would feel like an outsider.

When Sir John started to snore and no one was paying her any mind, she stuck her theoretical pillowcase under her chair and slipped out.

She should've gone to her chambers. There was that Regency rule that single women weren't supposed to walk out alone except in the morning, but Jane had a headache, and nothing goes worse with a headache than rules.

The night air sloshed on her bare skin and nudged her into shivering. Jane rubbed her arms and imagined Mrs. Wattlesbrook's voice crying out in Obi-Wan Kenobi tones: "Remember to wear a wrap and bonnet when you go out!" She half hoped that the old woman would find her now and just send her home and get it over with. But she was alone.

She wandered the garden path (so as not to get grass stains on her hem), and gave up a halfhearted hope that Colonel Andrews would come looking for her. Without hope, it was impossible to fantasize. That was her problem, Jane decided—she'd always lugged around an excess of hope. If only she were more of a pessimist, she wouldn't have to grapple with these impossible whimsies and wouldn't be here now, forlorn and pathetic in make-believe England.

She wound around with the path until she approached the smaller second building that housed the servants. A first-story window flickered with the unmistakable bluish light of a television set, and it drew her nearer, a moth to flame. She could hear an announcer burble "New York Knicks" and "Pacers," though she couldn't make out any details. The real, gritty, urban, twenty-first-century clamor of U.S. basketball sounded as good to her as chocolate soup.

That's right—she remembered now that those teams were opening the NBA season in a game on October 30, which meant if someone was watching it tonight in England they must have played yesterday in New York, making today—

"Halloween," she said aloud. "How appropriate."

The cold and the dark night rubbed against the blue light and the sound of the game, and the thought of going back alone to bed or returning to watch the whist game made her want to scream. She stepped up to the door and knocked.

The television voice cut off, replaced by the sound of pattering activity. "Just a moment," said a male voice.

The door opened. It was Martin, aka Theodore the gardener, in pajama pants and no top, a towel hanging around his neck. Unclothed, he had the kind of build that made her want to say, "Yow." She was glad she was wearing her favorite dress.

"Trick or treat?" she said.

"What?"

"Sorry to interrupt." She indicated the towel. "You're working out?"

"Miss, uh, Erstwhile, right? Yes, hello. No, I just couldn't find my shirt. Are you lost?"

"No, I was walking and I . . . I don't suppose you could give me the Knicks–Pacers score?"

Martin stared blankly for a moment, then looking around as if trying to spy out eavesdroppers, pulled her inside and shut the door behind her.

"You could hear that?"

"The TV? Yes, a little, and I saw the light through your window."

"Blasted paper-thin curtains." He grimaced and ran his fingers through his hair. "You are going to catch me at everything bad, aren't you? Let's hope you're not her spy. She'll have my balls for stew."

"Who, Mrs. Wattlesbrook?"

"Yes, in whose presence I signed a dozen nondisclosure and proper-behavior and first-child and I don't know what other kinds of promises, in one of which I swore to keep any modern thingies out of sight of the guests."

"Tell me that Wattlesbrook isn't her real name."

"It is, actually."

"Oh, no," she said with a laugh in her voice.

"Oh, yes." He sat on the edge of his bed. "I take it, then, you're not spying for her? Good. Yes, dear Mrs. Wattlesbrook, descended from the noble water buffalo. It's a decent job, though. Best pay for being a gardener I've ever had." He met her eyes. "I'd hate to lose it, Miss Erstwhile."

"I'm not going to tattletale," she said in tired big-sister tones. "And you can't call me Miss Erstwhile when you have a towel around your neck. To real people I'm Jane."

"I'm still Martin."

"How did you get the game on your TV out here, anyway?"

He jerked a sheet off a combination television and VCR with a magician's *ta-da* flourish, explaining that he'd asked a guy from the town to record it for him that afternoon.

"I know, Why risk so much for a basketball game? Behold the weakness that is man."

"Did you play basketball?" she asked, eyeing again his sleek height.

"Americans always ask me that, and so, curious, I started watching the NBA games a couple of years ago. Now I'm shamelessly addicted. They're a bit more exciting than football, aren't they? About as much running around but a lot more goals. Don't tell a soul from Sheffield that I said that. Long live the Manchester United."

"Yes, absolutely, go United," she said, crossing herself.

"So, uh, you came about the score."

"Yes, the score," she said, having forgotten all about it.

"Last I saw, it was fifteen to ten Knicks, first quarter."

"First quarter? Well, would you mind if I stayed and watched the rest?"

"If Mrs. Wattlesbrook finds you here . . ."

"They all think I'm in bed. No one will come looking for me. I'm last in precedence, after all."

They stripped his bed and hung the sheets and bedspread on the curtain rod for "extra blue-light protection," then turned the volume down so low they had to whisper not to drown out the announcer. She felt cozy and mischievous, watching the game in the dark apartment, hidden from that Mrs. Hannigan-of-a-proprietress, sipping a can of root beer from Martin's minifridge.

"You drink root beer while you watch an NBA game? You are an American wannabe, aren't you?"

"That is perhaps the most horrid thing you could say to an Englishman."

"Worse than French wannabe?"

"Well, there is that." He sipped his soda. "I spent a summer in America and one night drank two six-packs of root beer on a dare. After that, the formerly vile-cough-syrupy taste suddenly became appealing. But wait just a moment, Miss I've-Just-Come-From-A-Rather-Dull-Game-Of-Whist, who's pointing fingers and calling me a wannabe of anything?"

"Yeah . . ." She smoothed the front of her empire waist and laughed at herself as best she could. "It's, um, a Halloween costume. You know, trick or treat."

"Ah," he said. "And my interest in basketball is just, you know, research into a curious cultural phenomenon."

"Pure research."

"Absolutely."

"But of course. Besides, you ruined me, you know. No wonder Wattlesbrook forbids anything modern to clash with the nineteenth century. Five minutes of conversation with you in the garden and I went cross-eyed trying to take myself seriously again in this getup."

"I have that effect on a lot of women. All it takes is five minutes with me and—er . . . that didn't sound right."

"You'd better stop while you're behind, there, sport."

The television seemed to grow quieter, and they moved closer to it, from the couch to the carpet, and sitting on the floor with her corset still stiffening her back, she had to lean against him to be comfortable. And then his arm was around her shoulder, and his smell was delicious. She felt drunk on root beer, and soothed by the twitching of the tiny television. He started to play with her fingers, and she turned her head. Their breaths touched. Then their lips.

And then, they really made out.

It was fun, kissing a guy she barely knew. She'd never done this before, and it made her feel rowdy and pretty and miles removed from her issues. She didn't think or fret. She just played.

"Good shot," she said, her eyes closed, pretending to watch the game.

"Watch that defense," he whispered, kissing her neck. An evening dress allowed for a lot of neck, and somehow he got it all. "Get the rebound, you clumsy oaf."

And it was fun to stop kissing and look at each other, breathless, feeling the thrill and anticipation of the undone.

"Good game," she said.

The television buzzed with static. She didn't know how long the game had been over, but her heavy eyes and limbs told her that it was very late. She thought if she stayed longer, she would fall asleep on his chest, and because that idea pleased her, she left immediately. Her torso stiff inside her corset exoskeleton, he had to help her to her feet. With one hand, he pulled her onto her toes as though she were the weight of a pillow.

He walked her to the door and swatted her on the butt. "Good game, coach. See you tomorrow."

"Um, who won?" she asked, indicating the television still droning angrily at having no picture to show.

"We did."

Jane didn't know what hour it was, since a timepiece wasn't part of her wardrobe allotment, but the moon had moved considerably across the sky. Her arms bare below her thin sleeves, she shivered and crept across the courtyard, the whisper of the gravel path announcing her presence to any lurkers. She entered through the grand front door, clicking it closed behind her, and eased her slippers over the creaking boards.

It was strange creeping through that big house at night, and she had the itchy sensation of being watched or followed.

"Who's there?" she asked once, feeling very "Turn of the Screw." Did someone see her coming from Martin's? Would she be sent home? Would he be fired?

No one answered.

She locked her chamber door behind her and didn't bother to ring for Matilda as it was so late. It was impossible to do up her corset without help, but she had undressed alone, though somewhat awkwardly, on other occasions. Stripped to her chemise, she melted into the cool sheets. She could smell Martin on her hands, and she gleefully cozied into her pillows, enjoying the sensation of having recently been kissed.

Of course it meant nothing beyond the fun of it, because she'd given up on men and love, after all, and was quite firm with herself about hoping too much. But it had been nice. And a first for Jane—a harmless fling!

Tonight, Jane had been kissed. Tonight she thought, Mr. Darcy who?

Boyfriend #3

Dave Atters, AGE SIXTEEN

She really liked this one, the power forward on the high school varsity team and the beginning of her unhealthy infatuation with basketball. She giggled and sighed and dreamed. He said jump, and she leaped. But when he parked his spoiled-boy convertible in front of her house after a date and thrust his hand up her skirt, she pushed him away. When she wouldn't relent, he ordered her out of the car. At school, he acted as though they'd never met.

Years later, she considered seeing a therapist about this one until she realized that Dave "Fancy Hands" Atters wasn't the guy holding her back—the blame really lay with Fitzwilliam "I love you against my better judgment" Darcy. Besides, there'd been the night of Homecoming when she and Molly had spray-painted SHE-MALE on the side of Dave's convertible. That had been fairly therapeutic.

days 5–6

JANE COULD SCARCELY WAIT FOR night to come again. Social rules required that the ladies now visit Pembrook Cottage, and then Miss Heartwright had to be invited over to dine yet again. Jane had become the fourth woman in a three-gentleman household. Though the colonel's smiling eyes often sought her out, and she was able to flay Mr. Nobley verbally at dinner, her attention kept dancing to thoughts of bedspreads on the curtain rod, root beer and television, and a man who smelled of gardens. Something real.

After Martin's room, life in the drawing room seemed dulled and fuzzy—waiting for the gentlemen while chatting about nothing, welcoming the gentlemen and continuing to chat about nothing, every topic harmless and dry, everyone holding themselves a careful arm's distance away.

What a crock, she thought. What absolute boredom and inanity. It can't really have been like this. And if it was, why didn't all those Regency women go insane?

After a painfully long hour pressed into playing speculation, she declared she would retire and sneaked out to the servants' quarters.

She didn't intend to make out with Martin again. But she did anyway. He was so cute and funny and so-not-Mr.-Darcy. And she felt so light and silly and so-not-typical-Jane. What a last hurrah he was, this tall, coy Englishman who watched basketball. Nothing like her fantasy, nothing like anything she'd done before. She didn't once try to steer the conversation to the topic of whether he wanted one day to be a father (her oft-used test), and she wasn't even tempted to daydream about a wedding with that soaring figure by her side. A true miracle.

The next morning at breakfast, she looked at the gentlemen and felt proud, perhaps even smug. A house full of Regency dreamboats and she chose the root-beer-sipping gardener. Martin was appearing to be a serendipitous answer to her Darcy therapy.

The third night, by the time she'd arrived at Martin's apartment, his bedspread was already blocking the window, Stevie Wonder was playing on his CD player ("very superstitious"), and his bedside table was set up with a towel as a tablecloth and a Coke bottle full of fresh lavender.

"You mentioned your longing for familiar food," he said, and pulled out a McDonald's bag.

They ate the cold meat-product hamburgers and nearly potato-free fries by the light of television static, which had become to Jane more romantic than candles, and traded tragic childhood stories.

"I was twelve and my mom still wouldn't let me shave my legs," Jane said. "One night I stole her razor and shaved in bed. In the dark. Without soap."

"I was a punk kid, horribly skinny at age ten, and liked to throw eggs at cars. Yes, I know, the creativity of young boys is inspiring. I made the mistake of hitting the car of Gerald Lewis, the neighborhood's bodybuilding record holder, who still lived with his mum. He slung me up by my belt on a tree branch eight feet off the ground. I hung there for an hour."

Tonight she would definitely leave without so much as a good-bye kiss. She was in this for the company, after all. This was not a reality TV show where the producers, in attorney-approved speech, persuaded the bachelorette to make out with every hunk in the game. Then, as she stood against the door, her hand on the doorknob, he leaned over to kiss her cheek. The salty smell of man deluged her, and she leaped up to reach his lips, wrapping her legs around his middle, separated by oodles of skirt.

"How tall are you anyway?" she asked.

"About two hundred centimeters," he said, his glance flicking from her eyes to her lips. "Six-foot-six to you, Miss American Pie."

She held on to his neck and he held her against the door, kissing until they couldn't breathe. Making out with Martin was perhaps the most fun kissing she'd ever had. His hands seemed impatient, and she marveled at his ability to keep them out of the No Fly Zones. The result was the passion didn't escalate to frenzy. It was soft and ardent, the focus just on the kissing, just on the pressure of two bodies near, and the exhilarating restraint. For Jane, the thrill and danger felt like an extreme sport.

"You should probably go," he said.

"Mm-hm," she mumbled, her mouth on his, her hands investigating the girth of his chest.

She didn't want to go. He didn't want her to go, either. She could feel the eagerness in his hands, the speed of his breathing. He groaned regret, but he grabbed her waist and placed her back on her feet.

"As much as I hate to, I really should walk you to the door."

She laughed. She was already at the door—pressed against it, in fact. He turned the knob, letting in the drenched smell of night.

"Good night, Miss Erstwhile." He kissed her hand.

Jane went through the door backward as though she departed from the presence of a king, turned around, and found herself walking crooked.

The night was perfect, the darkness reclining smooth and full on the garden, as rich as a painting of a classical nude. The leaves churned above Jane's head. The pale snaking garden paths hinted at movement, at possibilities not seen. All the beauty of the cool autumn darkness seemed too much to comprehend, and her artist's instinct perked up. She told it to hush—now was not the

72

time to work out how to paint an English night. She was spinning from this unexpected find inside Austenland. A real man. A tall man! Someone to kiss and make her feel sexy and fun. Someone who didn't insist on more than she could give, who allowed her to live in perfect moments, who made her want to smile instead of fret about future what-ifs. For the first time in years, or perhaps ever, Ms. Jane Hayes felt . . . relaxed.

She plunged into bed and closed her eyes. And wondered how early she could slip away to see Martin again tomorrow.

Boyfriend #4

Ray Riboldi, AGE SEVENTEEN

Ray was pockmarked and didn't wash his hair every day, but it didn't matter, because he was nice. After boyfriends 2 and 3, Jane read Mansfield Park and decided that a kind, quiet guy was the way to go. Ray picked her wildflowers. He gave her the Hostess desserts his mother still packed him for lunch, even the fruit pies, and his constant gaze made her feel luscious.

After a couple of months, two guys Jane had grown up with decided Ray shouldn't be dating out of his Appearance Pool and played a prank involving catapulting dog poop (so original!) into the open roof of Ray's rusty Jeep.

"Stay away from girls too pretty for you!" they shouted, tires squealing out of the school parking lot.

Jane swore she wasn't involved, but Ray didn't listen. In the middle of the cafeteria, he ground a premeditated Hostess cupcake into her hair. Hard.

"How do you like it? Huh?"

Turned out, he wasn't that nice after all.

day 7

THE NEXT DAY WAS YET another late breakfast, reading in the morning room, a visit from Miss Heartwright, and a stroll with the gentlemen. The "stroll with gentlemen" part should've made Jane's hatted, sideburned fancies race, but she was disengaged now. Her eyes searched the garden for signs of that tall glass of water.

That afternoon she sat alone in the library, reading an Ann Radcliffe novel, *The Italian*, her brain straining to keep up with the archaic storytelling. Part of the Experience was the life of leisure, she knew, but she was an adopted New Yorker, an heiress to the Puritan work ethic, and doing next to nothing all day was taking its toll. She had begun to daydream of the oddest things: washing her clothes in the sink when all her building's laundry machines were occupied; the hot, human smell of a full subway; eating a banana from a street vendor; buying a disposable umbrella in a downpour.

All the hours she had spent daydreaming of living in Austen's world, and now here she was pondering the mundane realities of normal life. It seemed too cruel.

So she decided to hunt Martin down during the day. What was stopping her? After all, he wasn't a vampire.

It was pleasant and sunny, though as she strolled the flat, elegant garden, the glare soon made her want shade. The mazelike lines of low hedges were disrupted in the center by a miniature Parthenon that might have been placed, monolithesque, by meddling aliens. In her present mood, she found it unsettling, an obvious falsehood inside the otherwise natural loveliness of flowers and shrubs, turning the garden into a farce.

Jane spotted a couple gray, squat-hatted heads dispersed

through the wilderness areas of the park before discovering a tall gardener pruning growth by a low stone wall. She sat on the wall, opened her book, and paid him no mind. After a few minutes the sounds of clipping stopped, and she felt his gaze on her. She turned a page.

"Jane," he said with a touch of exasperation.

"Shh, I'm reading," she said.

"Jane, listen, someone warned me that another fellow heard my telly playing and told Mrs. Wattlesbrook, and I had to toss it out this morning. If they spot me hanging around you . . ."

"You're not hanging around me, I'm reading."

"Bugger, Jane . . ."

"Martin, please, I'm sorry about your TV but you can't cast me away now. I'll go raving mad if I have to sit in that house again all afternoon. I haven't sewn a thing since junior high Home Ec when I made a pair of gray shorts that ripped at the butt seam the first time I sat down, and I haven't played *pianoforte* since I quit from boredom at age twelve, and I haven't read a book in the middle of the day since college, so you see what a mess I'm in."

"So," Martin said, digging in his spade. "You've come to find me again when there is no one else to flirt with."

Huh! thought Jane.

He snapped a dead branch off the trunk.

Huh! she thought again. She stood and started to walk away.

"Wait." Martin hopped after her, grabbing her elbow. "I saw you with those actors, parading around the grounds this morning. I hadn't seen you with them before. In the context. And it bothered me. I mean, you don't really go in for this stuff, do you?"

Jane shrugged.

"You do?"

"More than I want to, though you've been making it seem unnecessary lately."

Martin squinted up at a cloud. "I've never understood the women who come here, and you're one of them. I can't make sense of it."

"I don't think I could explain it to a man. If you were a woman, all I'd have to say is 'Colin Firth in a wet shirt' and you'd say, 'Ah.'"

"Ah. I mean, aha! is what I mean."

Crap. She'd hoped he would laugh at the Colin Firth thing. And he didn't. And now the silence made her feel as though she were standing on a seesaw, waiting for the weight to drop on the other side.

Then she smelled it. The musty, acrid, sour, curdled, metallic, decaying odor of ending. This wasn't just a first fight. She'd been in this position too many times not to recognize the signs.

"Are you breaking up with me?" she asked.

"Were we ever together enough to require breaking up?"

Oh. Ouch. She took a step back on that one. Perhaps it was her dress that allowed her to compose herself more quickly than normal. She curtsied.

"Pardon the interruption, I mistook you for someone I knew."

She turned and left, wishing for a Victorian-type gown so she could have whipped the full skirts for a satisfying little cracking sound. She had to satisfy herself with emphatically tightening her bonnet ribbon as she marched.

You stupid, stupid girl, she thought. You were fantasizing again. Stop it!

It had all been going so well. She'd let herself have fun, unwind, not plague a new romance with constant questions such as, What if? And after? And will he love me forever?

"Are you breaking up with me . . . ?" she muttered to herself. He must think she was a lunatic. And really, he'd be right. Here she was in Pembrook Park, a place where women hand over scads of dough to hook up with men paid to adore them, but she finds the one man on campus who's in a position to reject her and then leads him into it. Typical Jane.

Boyfriend #5

Rahim (last name forgotten),

AGE "THIRTY-FIVE" (POSSIBLY FORTY+)

"You are so lovely," he told Jane across the perfume counter. She was nineteen, in college, making minimum wage, and she'd just had the worst haircut in her life. Possibly that's why his compliment felt more important than it was, a gorgeous bird she couldn't bear to let go.

For three weeks he took her to restaurants, expensive restaurants, and he paid! In a spree of crazy extravagance, she ordered appetizers and dessert. Then one night he lured her to his apartment, which smelled like oil. Body oil. The kind that pools on skin that hasn't seen a shower for a week.

With his eyes half closed, his hand mauled her shoulder, and he said, "I want to make love to you," in a clumsy swat at romance. She thought of the moment Elizabeth runs into Mr. Darcy at Pemberley; by comparison, Rahim's slippery pawing made Jane laugh. Out loud.

There was an excruciating pause. She cleared her throat and mumbled an apology as she left.

JANE WORE HER LEAST FAVORITE evening dress to dinner, the green one with the brown trimming that fit like a tent. It didn't matter. Martin wouldn't see her, or anyone else for that matter, as she trudged along at the rear end of the precedence beast. She thought she hid her gloom well, and then she got tired of hiding it. In the drawing room, she grabbed a book and slumped as best as her corset would allow.

"Do sit down to cards with us this evening, Miss Erstwhile," Miss Heartwright said as the gentlemen joined them in the drawing room. "I can't bear to have you reading alone again."

Jane wanted to glare. Miss Heartwright, even when sitting straight with a Regency woman's wood-plank spine, maintained an effortless manner, as though she were simply lounging against the sturdiness of her own perfection. And then there was that twinkle in her eye and her impossibly white teeth. Maddening.

"No, thank you." Jane was in no mood to banter.

"Come, you must. Mr. Nobley," Miss Heartwright said, turning to her favorite of the gentlemen, "help me persuade Miss Erstwhile out of her tortoise shell."

Mr. Nobley glanced up from his book. "If Miss Erstwhile wishes to read rather than play, I will not provoke her."

"Thank you, Mr. Nobley," said Jane, and she meant it.

He nodded, as though they were co-conspirators. It was a disconcerting gesture from that man.

"Mr. Nobley," Miss Heartwright intoned with the sweetest of smiles, "you at least I can entice for a short round of speculation."

For her, Mr. Nobley put down his book and joined the card table. The sight of it made Jane declare she would retire early. This time she stopped in her chamber for her pelisse and bonnet.

It was a relief to be outdoors. In the chill and dark, the world seemed closer, intimate. She shivered and walked until her blood warmed and helped her fight the ache of vulnerability. She wished for Molly, a best friend who'd laugh with her over her Martin mistake and loyally find Jane faultless and everyone else in the wrong.

She'd meant to avoid the servants' quarters, really she had, but she was lost in imaginings of some sort of violently gorgeous triumph—she'd be the prettiest one at the ball, all the actors would *really* fall in love with her, and she'd say no to them all and leave Pembrook Park a whole woman who buries all her teenage fantasies in one fell swoop . . . And she came upon Martin's window, dark as the sky. No, there was a flicker, a gray haze of light. Did he have the bedspread up? Did he get a new television? Should she knock and apologize for being freak-out Jane and see if they could start over again or just skip to the making out part? In her current state—jilted in England and wearing Regency dress—Jane found she had a difficult time rating that proposal on her list of all-time bad ideas.

The quiet and cold washed over her, and she stood by his window, waiting for a decision to bite her. In some tree, a bird croaked a suggestion. Jane wished she spoke Bird.

"What are you doing?"

"Ya!" said Jane, whirling around, her hands held up menacingly.

It was Mr. Nobley with coat, hat, and cane, watching her with wide eyes. Jane took several quick (but oh so casual) steps away from Martin's window.

"Um, did I just say, 'Ya'?"

"You just said 'Ya,'" he confirmed. "If I am not mistaken, it was a battle cry, warning that you were about to attack me."

"I, uh . . ." She stopped to laugh. "I wasn't aware until this precise and awkward moment that when startled in a strange place, my instincts would have me pretend to be a ninja."

Mr. Nobley put the back of his hand to his mouth to cough. Or was it really a laugh? No, Mr. Nobley had no sense of humor.

"Excuse me, then, I probably have a secret mission somewhere." She started to walk past him toward the house, but he grabbed her arm to stop her.

"Wait just a moment, please." He looked around as if making sure they weren't observed, then led her rather forcefully to the side of the house where the moon and lamplight did not touch them.

"Let go!"

He did. "Miss Erstwhile, I believe it is in your best interest to tell me what you are doing out here."

"Walking." She glared. She did not particularly enjoy being dragged by her arm.

His eyes darted to the servants' quarters. To Martin's exact window. It made her swallow.

"You are not doing something foolish, are you?"

In fact, she was, but that didn't mean she had to stop glaring.

"I don't know if you realize," he said in his unbearably condescending tone, "but it is not proper for a lady to be out alone after dark and worse to cavort with servants . . ."

"Cavort?"

"When doing so might lead to trouble of the worst nature . . ."

"Cavort?"

"Look," he said, slipping into slightly more colloquial tones, "just stay away from there."

"Aren't you all righteous concern, Mr. Nobley? Five minutes ago, I'd planned on changing careers and becoming a dairymaid, but you've saved me from that fate. I'll kindly release you back to the night and return to my well-bred ways."

"Don't be a fool, Miss Erstwhile." He returned the way he'd come, from the back of the house.

"Insufferable," she said under her breath.

No, she wasn't going to go to Martin's, curse him, but she wasn't going to run back to her room either, if just to spite Mr. Nobley. The man deserved to be spited. Or spitted. Or both. Though boring and cold and hateful, Mr. Nobley *was* the most Darcy-esque of them all, so she despised him with vigorous enthusiasm. Perhaps, she hoped, the exercise would count toward therapy and her ultimate Austenland recovery.

"Grab my arm, will he?" she said, getting a speck of satisfaction by muttering like an old crazy woman. "Call *me* a fool . . ."

She walked around the park in angry circles. Her fingers were cold, and her thoughts wandered to memories of spending so much time in the bath as a kid that her fingertips crinkled like raisin skin. Wrinkly skin reminded her of Great-Aunt Carolyn, with her extravagantly soft fingers and conspiratorial eyes.

She bought me this gift, Jane thought. Use it well, you floppy-brained, hopeless idiot, and stop trying to fall in love with gardeners. With anyone.

The night drew back, large and empty, no longer lying against her skin. She felt really alone now. But here's the thing—suddenly, she felt as though she belonged inside the aloneness, and that feeling made her whisper aloud, "I never have before. I've never felt at home with myself."

She looked at the servants' quarters and had Realization #2: She truly didn't want to go to Martin's. She hadn't earlier. It was just habit. In the past she was always ready to limp back after being rejected, hopeful to be scooped up again. But now, here, she lost the desire utterly.

"Ha!" she said to the night.

With a shift in the wind and a swish of her quiet skirt, she felt her mission at Austenland begin to change. This was no last hurrah before accepting spinsterhood—oh no. (And what a relief!) This was going to be *immersion therapy*. Martin had helped her see one thing, at least—she still liked men, a whole lot, in fact, and ain't nothing gonna change that. She just needed to screw her head on straight so that she could properly enjoy being young and female and as beautiful as she wanted to be.

She turned her back to the servants' quarters and faced the house as she used to look at the goal on her high school basketball court. Her new objective was to drown herself in the ridiculousness of her fantasy, a task like eating nothing but chocolate until she couldn't bear the thought of eating something sweet again. Get it out of her system. See for certain that this wouldn't really make her happy. Then she'd be her own woman again. Only two weeks left to make it happen. But she had to plunge in headfirst, she had to really try, or sure as her houseplants were at that moment gasping their last breath, one day she would look back at the experience and unsettle herself with wondering, What if? And, What if?

When night was definite and all housemates surely abed, Jane creaked open the front door, welcomed by the homey scent of floor wax. A light in the drawing room startled her, and she wondered if the group was playing some Olympian round of cards. But the room was deserted. Two lamps burned away the darkness.

On the table lay the book Mr. Nobley had been reading, and she leafed through its pages, wondering what sort of irritating story would fascinate that man's mind. A piece of paper slipped out, floating to the carpet. It was a pay stub made out to a Henry Jenkins with an address in Brighton. Was this Mr. Nobley? She stuck the paper back and laid it beside the nearly empty crystal decanter that was Sir John Templeton's dearest friend. Out of curiosity, Jane lifted the cap and sniffed, expecting a sugary punch smell to satisfy her suspicions. Nope, definitely alcohol. She was surprised—how could the actor keep up the virtual drinking and not get literally toasted?

As in answer to her thought, the man himself loomed in the doorway. She startled and dropped the decanter cap on the carpet.

"Well, good evening, Miss Erssssstwhile," Sir John said, dragging out the snake sound of her name. "Are you still a Miss or were you a Miss *erstwhile*, hm?"

"Yes, that's clever. Um, you startled me, Sir John."

"Up late, are you? Where did you go tonight? Up to some mischief, I hope."

"I just needed some air. Now if you'll excuse me . . ."

"Hmm." He leaned against the doorjamb and seemed to doze for a moment. Jane replaced the cap, clicked off the fake-kerosene lamps, and tried to slip past Sir John without rousing him. But just a few steps down the dark hallway, she felt a hot breath against her neck.

"Stay a moment."

Jane turned around with some apprehension, but she did stay. She had decided to play this game out, and with her personal story at Pembrook Park waning, she didn't want to pass up any plot twist he might be offering.

"What is it, Sir John?"

"I just thought we might spend a moment alone together, perhaps engage in our own private game of," he leaned closer to her face, "whissst."

She coughed once. "That's a four-person game."

"If you like. But I thought we could be partners. A little wink-wink, a little nudge-nudge under the table, you understand me?"

She sorted through the Austen plots searching for a scenario when a married man solicits a young lady. There was the doomed tryst in *Mansfield Park* with married lady and bachelor, but Sir John was no—what was his name?—no suave young Henry Crawford.

"I think I should go to bed," she said, unsure of how he was expecting her to proceed but not enjoying the game.

"Precisely my point," he said.

He began to advance again. She stepped back until she hit the wall.

"Hold on, now," she said, stopping him with a hand on his chest.

Sir John took her hand and held it in both of his own. His skin was hot and scratchy.

"You are so, so lovely." His breath hit her again, and she gagged at the stench of food and fermentation. He was clearly much drunker than she'd suspected.

"Sir John, you're married."

"Not really," he said, winking. Or perhaps, blinking poorly. "Me and the missus sleep in separate beds, don't tell her I told you, and I have been so lonely, lonely and cold, cold like your sweet hands. And we never had a specimen so young and pretty and taut as yourself."

She tried to push him away, but he pushed her back, pinning her against the wall. A lamp fixture above her rattled at the impact. His hands held both of hers, his round belly pressed against her, his mouth leered near her own.

"Surely a young beauty like yourself is lonely, too. It can be a part of the game, if you like."

"Get off," she said, thoroughly done with this.

His answer was to lean in closer. So she kneed him in the groin. As hard as she could.

"Aw, ow, dammit!" He doubled over and thudded onto his knees.

Jane brushed off her knee, feeling like it had touched something dirty. "Aw, ow, dammit indeed! What're you thinking?"

Jane heard hurried footsteps coming down the stairs. It was Mr. Nobley.

"Miss Erstwhile!" He was barefoot in his breeches, his shirt untucked. He glanced down at the groaning man. "Sir John!"

"Ow, she kicked me," said Sir John.

"Kneed him, I kneed him," Jane said. "I don't kick. Not even when I'm a ninja."

Mr. Nobley stood a moment in silence, looking over the scene. "I hope you remembered to shout 'Ya' when taking him down. I hear that is very effective."

"I'm afraid I neglected that bit, but I'll certainly 'ya' from here to London if he ever touches me again."

"Miss Erstwhile, were you perhaps employed by your president's armed forces in America?"

"What? Don't British women know how to use their knees?"

"Happily, I have never put myself in a position to find out." He stared at the prostrate Sir John. "Did he hurt you?"

"Frankly, your arm-yanking earlier was worse."

"I see. Perhaps you should retire to your chambers, Miss Erstwhile. Would you like me to escort you?"

"I'm fine," she said, "as long as there aren't any other Sir Johns lurking upstairs."

"Well, I cannot give Colonel Andrews a glowing reference, but I believe the way is safe."

She stepped closer to Mr. Nobley and whispered, "Are you going to out me to Mrs. Wattlesbrook for the servants' quarters lurking?"

"I think," he said, nudging the prostrate Sir John with his foot, "that you have suffered enough tonight."

Mr. Nobley smiled at her, the first time she had seen his real smile. She wouldn't go so far as to call it a grin. His lips were closed, but his eyes brightened and the corners of his mouth definitely turned up, creating pleasing little cheek wrinkles on either side as though the smile were in parentheses. It bothered her in a way she couldn't explain, like feeling itchy but not knowing exactly where to scratch. He was not particularly amused, she saw, but smiled to reassure her. Wait, who wanted to reassure her? Mr. Nobley or the actual man, Actor X?

"Thanks. Good night, Mr. Nobley."

"Good night, Miss Erstwhile."

She hesitated, then left, Sir John's groans following her up the stairs. On the second floor, Aunt Saffronia was emerging from her room, clutching a white shawl over her nightgown.

"What was that noise? Is everything all right?"

"Yes. It was . . . your husband. He was being inappropriate."

Aunt Saffronia blinked. "Inebriated?"

"Yes."

She nodded slowly. "I'm sorry, Jane."

Jane wasn't sure if Aunt Saffronia was speaking to Jane the niece or Jane the client. For the first time it didn't matter; both Janes felt exactly the same. She acknowledged the apology with a nod, went to her room, and locked the door behind her. She thought she was angry but instead she plopped herself down on her bed, put her face in her pillow, and laughed.

"What a joke," she said, sounding to herself like the movie incarnation of Lydia Bennet. "I come for Mr. Darcy, fall for the gardener, and get propositioned by the drunk husband."

Tomorrow would be different. Tomorrow she would play for real. She was going to drive full force into the game, have a staggering good time, and kick the nasty Darcy habit for good. She fell asleep with the ticklish thought of Mr. Nobley's smile.

Boyfriend #6

Josh Lake, AGE TWENTY

They met when two large groups of friends bumped and merged at the college carnival fundraiser, "Fifty Acres of Fun!" Somehow Jane got strapped together with perfect-stranger Josh and semiacquaintance Britney in the "Drop 'n' Swing," only the "drop" function malfunctioned, and the three of them hung facedown, harnessed to the tip of the twelve-story steel tower for fifteen minutes. Britney went nuts, cussing at the scrambling carnival workers, red faced, spit falling 150 feet. When Jane told her to take it easy, Britney's angry fear knew no bounds. She unleashed her longshoreman vocabulary on Jane and Josh, which made them laugh so hard that when the sudden, stomach-prying drop finally occurred, they had no breath to scream.

So potent was the bond formed at 150 feet, it took Jane three months of inept kisses and conversations poking at subjects of minimal philosophical depth ("But really, Jane, think about it—if libraries close at nine P.M., how will the nocturnal underprivileged ever advance? I mean, think about it!") to finally say,

"We should probably just break up."

He shrugged. "Yeah, okay."

Way to put up a fight, Josh.

day 8

JANE TOOK THE MORNING SLOWLY, as all Regency and recently scorned women must. She lay on her stomach in bed, sticking her feet in the air with pointed toes, taking comfort in feeling girly, and played with her cell phone. With that device in her hand, she felt an uncanny thrill of power, a time traveler gifted with secret future technology. It was a weapon, and she had questions to attack. Still, phoning Molly felt too scandalous, too rule-breaking, and she was determined to dive into Austenland headfirst. But a brief e-mail to her journalist friend felt just fine:

Hey chica, Need bckgrnd chk. Martin Jasper, Bristol/Sheffield. Also Henry Jenkins, Brighton. Miss you. This place bizarre and fun. Wll hv stories to tell. J.

A peek at her in-box reminded her how piteously dull the real world can be, so Jane began to play Bubble Master, an addicting strategy game for long subway rides. She had not been at it fifteen minutes (with a record high score of 582 points!) when her maid came barging in for their daily round of strapping-Jane-into-her-corset. Jane thrust the phone under her pillow.

The gentlemen were not present to break their fast. With just three ladies clinking the flatware and chewing honey cakes and current cakes, the breakfast room was tense.

"Sir John was not feeling himself last night," said Aunt

Saffronia, her eyes flicking from plate to Jane and back to plate, "so Mr. Nobley offered to accompany him to see an apothecary in town, and Colonel Andrews went as well, having some business to attend to there. They are so attentive, such honest, caring lads. I shall feel their loss when they leave."

"I feel it today." Miss Charming pursed her lips. "Eating breakfast with no gentlemen and that Heartwright girl poaching on my men—this isn't what I was promised." She looked at Aunt Saffronia with the eye of a haggler.

Aunt Saffronia placed her hands in her lap, a calming gesture. "I know, my dear, but they will be back, and in the meantime . . ."

"I didn't come here for the meantime. I came for the men."

Poor Aunt Saffronia! Jane felt for her. She put a hand on Miss Charming's arm. "Lizzy, maybe you and I could go visit the stables and go for a ride or—"

"Not today, Jane. My feelings are hurt." A tear formed in one eye. "I was promised certain things about this place and I can tell you one thing—so far, no one's made me feel *enchanting*."

"Oh, my," Aunt Saffronia said, "I can't have unhappiness at my table. Spoils the digestion. Miss Charming, what say we call on Mrs. Wattlesbrook? I believe she would be very concerned to hear of any dissatisfaction during your visit."

Miss Charming looked at Aunt Saffronia with her dry eye, like a goose considering biting, then nodded her head and said, "Done."

Jane thought, Mrs. Wattlesbrook will have Mr. Nobley tamed into Charming's personal pet by sundown.

He'd been Miss Charming's choice from the beginning, though he'd quickly proved too much work to keep the woman's interest. He was the most eye-catching, no question, and he gave the appearance of having some real depth, if he'd just relax a bit.

Jane was curious to see how he changed once Wattlesbrook ordered him to charm Miss Charming. And that would be fine by Jane. So what that he'd come (needlessly) running to her rescue in his shirttails? The way he'd said, "Don't be a fool, Miss Erstwhile," made her want to poke him in the eye. He was supposed to be Darcy-adorable, not teeth-grindingly maddening.

After the ladies left, Jane read in the library, then in the morning room, then in the false summer of the conservatory, the dry tips of leaves whispering to her neck, tickling her to irritation. She did *not* want to stroll the park yet again, thank you. So, bored to desperate measures, she called on Pembrook Cottage.

It was a brisk five-minute walk down a gravel path, her parasol draping her in a perfect circle of shade. The November morning was chilly and damp and filled the air with ideas of harvest and pumpkins and trick-or-treating in a scratchy ballerina costume completely engulfed by a ski parka. It made Jane wistful.

Pembrook Cottage was built of the same yellow bricks as the main house, though much smaller with only a ground floor and four facing windows. The garden around it was idyllic, low-hanging apple trees bearing a few late-season offerings, a few clumps of blue asters still poking through the tangles of grass. It was the kind of house you dreamed about renting for a summer, a place you'd run to, sit down in a comfortable chair, and let out a sigh of relief.

Then Jane spied Miss Heartwright through the window, doing embroidery in the cottage's only sitting room while her mother, Mrs. Heartwright, snored in a chair. The old lady had also been asleep the first time Jane had called on the cottage with the other Pembrook ladies. Miss Heartwright looked up from her embroidery at the opposite wall, and Jane caught a glimpse of her face—the look in her eyes warned of panicked boredom. Jane nearly ran away before pity for the poor woman drove her to knock at the door.

Besides, Jane thought, I'm in the game for real now, and this is what a Regency woman would do. Even elitist Emma made house calls.

A red-cheeked maid led her into the sitting room to a chair by the fire and pleasantries were exchanged.

"Oh, thank you for calling, Miss Erstwhile!" Miss Heartwright said many times. And somehow that wasn't irritating. The lovely lady was positively glowing.

"Why do you . . . ?" Jane had been about to ask why Miss Heartwright put up with this drab little existence. Surely with the money she was paying and the status of Ideal Client, she could be a guest in the main house—but Jane knew such questions were forbidden. Likely Mrs. Heartwright was only faking the snore and listened keenly for any illegal tidbits to pass on to the proprietress. But, man, that snore sure sounded real. Then again, maybe she was some poor, senile old lady from a nearby village who had no idea what was going on. It would be like Mrs. Wattlesbrook to fool the lady's family into paying for her stay in an authentic nineteenth-century nursing home.

Jane cleared her throat. "That is to say, how do you fare today, Miss Heartwright?"

They chitchatted—weather (breezy and damp), the gentlemen's hunting (pheasants), news (Sir John at the apothecary's, the topic of gravest concern). Jane thought she understood why Austen often left these conversations up to the narrator and spared the reader the grotesquerie of having to follow it word by word.

After a lapse, Jane hemmed for something else to say.

"So, would you like to come up to the main house? We could wait for the gentlemen's return and inquire after the state of Sir John at the earliest possible—"

"Yes!" Miss Heartwright hopped up.

Jane was pretty sure Miss Heartwright's enthusiasm lay not in concern for the drunken husband but in the chance to hobnob with Mr. Nobley.

Ick, thought Jane, as she realized she was turning out to be poor Fanny Price in *Mansfield Park*—the plain girl, the lower-class girl, the one with no one to take her arm. Just now she wouldn't turn down that naughty nugget, Henry Crawford.

They strolled up to the main house, gravel crunching beneath their boots, wind teasing their bonnet strings.

"I'm sure my aunt will ask you to stay to dinner," Jane said.

"I hope so. Mama will be fine alone with Hillary, and I enjoy the company of everyone at Pembrook Park so well. Particularly you, Miss Jane." She took her arm. "I hope we are good friends."

If Miss Heartwright were any less perfect, that would have sounded laughable. But since she was flawless, it was merely exasperating. In an endearing way, of course.

A carriage coming up the drive spared Jane a reply. "That must be Aunt Saffronia and Miss Charming. Make haste," Jane added, just because she'd always wanted to say that.

Amazing how the sight of any moving object was exciting when one lived in such a stifled existence. They hurried (in a reserved, proper manner) to greet the carriage as it stopped before the house, then they were stopped in turn by the sight of a stranger emerging from the door of the carriage.

Miss Heartwright dropped Jane's arm and took a step back. Apparently, he wasn't a stranger to her.

The man was six-foot-two or taller, broad, deliciously manly, and dark-haired. He had a pleasant farm boy appeal to him, though he also seemed at ease in his gold-trimmed blue uniform. What a perfect way to start her true Austenland immersion! Jane hoped that he was single—that the character he played was single—whatever.

He stood there, waiting, looking at the horizon. If Miss Heartwright knew him, society rules said he couldn't speak to her unless she acknowledged him first, and then it would be up to her to introduce him to Jane.

Miss Heartwright was examining the gravel.

Jane nudged her. "Are you two acquaintances?"

"Oh, yes, forgive me. Miss Erstwhile, may I present Mr. George East? Mr. East, this is Miss Jane Erstwhile, niece to Sir and Lady Templeton."

Mr. East bowed. He did it very well.

"How do you do, Miss Erstwhile. I am Captain East."

"Captain?" Miss Heartwright's voice squeaked.

Their eyes met, then they both looked away. My, it was awkward.

"Oh," Jane said, remembering how Aunt Saffronia had spoken of a jilted man in Miss Heartwright's past. And here he was, and captained now, apparently. "Oh, I mean, I shouldn't keep you standing in the drive after your journey. My aunt is away, but please come in and sit with us."

Was that right? Could two unmarried ladies be alone with a single man? Jane couldn't remember for sure, but neither protested, so they sat in the sitting room, since that's what it was for. Jane asked a maid to bring in tea (and felt pretty cool being the lady of the house for the moment) and very soon she and Captain East were having a lively conversation while Miss Heartwright, unusually quiet, sat still and straight in a chair.

"So there we were," said the captain, "one lone British ship surrounded by four French war crafts, no help in sight. The captain dead on the deck, the crew terrified. 'Surrender!' came the shout in that grating French accent. 'Never!' said I. I will admit to you, Miss Erstwhile, I was very much tempted, but I had to hearten my men. 'Never!' said I."

"But why wouldn't you?" asked Jane, trying her hand at being the eager woman hearing of the wide world from an adventuresome man. "There could be no dishonor in that, with the captain dead and your men so outnumbered."

Captain East paused, looked at his hands, the remembrance of fake battles struggling beautifully across his actor's brow. "I had watched my courageous captain in a similar circumstance. He had said, 'When my British heart tells me what I must do, I do not fear to follow it through.'"

"Excuse me." Miss Heartwright stood, a book tumbling from her lap. "I must go see how Mama is doing." And she left in a hurry.

Captain East stood as well, as the Rules were pretty clear that he and Jane should not be together unchaperoned.

"I'll call Matilda to show you to your room, Captain."

"Thank you." He smiled, taking in her face. "It is, Miss Erstwhile, a pleasure to make your acquaintance."

When Matilda led him away, Jane announced to the empty room, "If you're listening, Big Brother, I refuse to be Fanny Price."

Paul Diaz, TWENTY-SOMETHING

He was in her watercolor class, so cute and the sweet kind of shy. They obviously clicked, the attraction thrilling between them, inspiring her to relish the infatuation freshman-style and write his name in her notebook in curvy, flowery script. She gave him openings but guessed he was too timid to ask her out. The day after finals, she ran into him at the deli on campus and thought she had nothing to lose.

"My work is having this fancy dinner party next weekend, the food's supposed to be great. Would you like to go with me?"

"Oh, uh, maybe, I'll have to check," he said. Then, "What was your name again?"

There's always something to lose.

day 8, continued

THAT NIGHT, THE PRECEDENCE WALK from drawing room to dining was in upheaval.

"Let me see," Aunt Saffronia said, catching herself before she chewed on a fingernail. "Mr. Nobley, would you be so kind as to take my arm? Colonel Andrews, would you escort Miss Charming? And Captain East (so happy to hear of your promotion, my dear! And much deserved, I am certain), if you will accompany Miss Heartwright, I believe you two know each other. Jane dear, you are certain you do not mind coming along alone? I can dine in my boudoir, if you prefer? No? Sir John extends his apologies for not returning to the Park, but he plans to stay in town to be near the apothecary until at least two weeks hence, poor man, so I am afraid you may not see him again before departing. Well, now that is settled, shall we dine?"

All through the soup, game bird, fish, fruit, and walnut courses, and later in the drawing room, Jane flirted madly (in a guarded, Regency sort of way) with Colonel Andrews, who was invigorated by the attention. It quickly became clear that Miss Heartwright was uninterested in her former acquaintance, so Jane added Captain East to her list of men-to-bat-eyelashes-at. Mr. Nobley was off-limits now, she supposed. He certainly seemed to be Miss Heartwright's darling. But after Miss Charming's visit to Mrs. Wattlesbrook's customer-complaint desk, she was sure to get priority over the man of her choice. Perhaps the two ladies would fight over him. Pembrook Park was pining for a hearty ladies' mud wrestle.

Jane, the captain, and the colonel begged out of cards, sat by the window, and made fun of Mr. Nobley. She glanced once at the garden, imagined Martin seeing her now, and felt popular and pretty—Emma Woodhouse from curls to slippers. It certainly helped that all the men were so magnificent. Unreal, actually. Austenland was feeling cozier.

"Do you think he hears us?" Jane asked. "See how he doesn't lift his eyes from that book? In all, his manners and expression are a bit *too* determined, don't you think?"

"Right you are, Miss Erstwhile," Colonel Andrews said.

"His eyebrow is twitching," Captain East said gravely.

"Why, so it is, Captain!" the colonel said. "Well observed."

"Then again, the eyebrow twitch could be caused by some buried guilt," Jane said.

"I believe you're right again, Miss Erstwhile. Perhaps he does not hear us at all."

"Of course I hear you, Colonel Andrews," said Mr. Nobley, his eyes still on the page. "I would have to be deaf not to, the way you carry on."

"I say, do not be gruff with us, Nobley, we are only having a bit of fun, and you are being rather tedious. I cannot abide it when my friends insist on being scholarly. The only member of our company who can coax you away from those books is our Miss Heartwright, but she seems altogether too pensive tonight as well, and so our cause is lost."

Mr. Nobley did look up now, just in time to catch Miss Heartwright's face turn away shyly.

"You might show a little more delicacy around the ladies, Colonel Andrews," he said.

"Stuff and nonsense. I agree with Miss Erstwhile, you are acting like a scarecrow. I do not know why you put on this act, Nobley, when around the port table or out in the field you're rather a pleasant fellow."

"Really? That is curious," Jane said. "Why, Mr. Nobley, are you generous in your attentions with gentlemen and yet taciturn and withdrawn around the fairer sex?"

Mr. Nobley's eyes were back on the printed page, though they didn't scan the lines. "Perhaps I do not possess the type of conversation that would interest a lady."

"You say 'perhaps' as though you do not believe it yourself. What else might be the reason, sir?" Jane smiled. Needling

Mr. Nobley was feeling like a very productive use of the evening.

"Perhaps another reason might be that I myself do not find the conversation of ladies to be very stimulating." His eyes were dark.

"Hm, I just can't imagine why you're still unmarried."

"I might say the same for you."

"Mr. Nobley!" cried Aunt Saffronia.

"No, it's all right, Aunt," Jane said. "I asked for it. And I don't even mind answering." She put a hand on her hip and faced him. "One reason why I am unmarried is because there aren't enough men with guts to put away their little boy fears and commit their love and stick it out."

"And *perhaps* the men do not *stick it out* for a reason."

"And what reason might that be?"

"The reason is women." He slammed his book shut. "Women make life impossible until the man has to be the one to end it. There is no working it out past a certain point. How can anyone work out the lunacy?"

Mr. Nobley took a ragged breath, then his face went red as he seemed to realize what he'd said, where he was. He put the book down gently, pursed his lips, cleared his throat.

No one in the room made eye contact.

"Someone has *issues*," said Miss Charming in a quiet, singsongy voice.

"I beg you, Lady Templeton," Colonel Andrews said, standing, his smile almost convincingly nonchalant, "play something rousing on the pianoforte. I promised to engage Miss Erstwhile in a dance. I cannot break a promise to such a lovely young thing, not and break her heart and further blacken her view of the world, so you see my urgency."

"An excellent suggestion, Colonel Andrews," Aunt Saffronia

said. "It seems all our spirits could use a lift. I think we feel the lack of Sir Templeton's presence, indeed I do."

Mr. Nobley, of course, declined to dance, so Jane and the colonel stood up with Captain East and Miss Charming, whose spirits were speedily improving. Twice she turned the wrong way, ramming herself into the captain's shoulder, saying "pip, pip," and "jolly good." Jane spied Mr. Nobley on the sofa, staring at the window and a reflection of the dancers.

At the next song, the couples switched partners, and though Captain East was not so fun and witty as the colonel, lacking that wicked glint that Jane found appealing despite herself, he was, frankly, gorgeous in a Clark-Kent-sans-glasses way. And such a sure dancer. And made her feel petite and girlish when he put a hand on her waist to promenade between the other couple. It was a scrumptious experience just to be touched, her Regency skin starved for intimacy, her real skin still missing Martin's fingers. The scurrilous beast.

"We're so happy you've come to visit, Captain East," said Jane.

"So am I. Indeed I am."

Was he for her, then? Could Mrs. Wattlesbrook have a soft heart after all? He would be a very good sort of brick wall to beat her head against and knock the Mr. Darcy nonsense out. He would also be a fine sight on her arm on strolls through the garden, should Martin happen to glance her way.

At the end of that song, gentleman that he was, Captain East went to Miss Heartwright, alone and downcast on the sofa.

"Miss Heartwright, would it please you to dance?"

It seemed obvious to Jane that Miss Heartwright would not be pleased, but she stood up with the captain anyway. What was their story? Sometimes Miss Heartwright seemed like Fanny Price, sometimes like Jane Bennet or Jane Fairfax, sometimes like Anne Elliot.

"I would beg a second dance with you, Miss Charming," said the colonel. "You do live up to your name!"

"Oh, go on," said Miss Charming.

The way Miss Charming was blushing now—real, honest blushing, not faking—it seemed she'd made her choice, and her choice wasn't Mr. Nobley. And so Jane was left neatly on the sidelines again. She didn't mind. Seriously she didn't. Okay, maybe just a little. After all, tonight was the most fun she'd had since she'd come.

"Miss Erstwhile?" Mr. Nobley was beside her suddenly. "It would seem my gentlemanly duty to ask you to dance."

She glanced at his hand. "You're still holding your book, Mr. Nobley."

He set it on a table, put one arm behind his back, and held the other out to her.

She sighed. "I'm sorry I pestered you back there, but I'd rather not dance for duty."

His hand extended toward her. "But it would be my honor."

She rolled her eyes but took his hand. The first time he touched her waist, she started. There was nothing passive in his touch, nothing wasted. She was aware of his hands the way she was often conscious of his gaze seeking her out. It was, to say the least, surprising.

With only three couples, they kept in fairly constant motion. As a general rule, conversation is more intimate in a crowd, but among only six people, every word, and silence, became public.

Colonel Andrews: "What a lovely gown, Miss Charming! You wear it well, or should I say, it wears you?"

Miss Charming: "Oh, you rascal!"

Miss Erstwhile: "Do you know the name of this tune, Mr. Nobley?"

Mr. Nobley: "I do not. It is a country tune."

Captain East: . . .

Miss Heartwright: . . .

Colonel Andrews: "I beg your pardon, Miss Charming. I seem to have stuck my foot under yours yet again."

Miss Charming: "Spit spot!"

Miss Erstwhile: "It is such a relief, Mr. Nobley, to already know that you find this exercise vulgar and your partner unworthy. It saves us the idle chitchat."

Mr. Nobley: "And yet you chat away."

Aunt Saffronia: "Lovely dance! Shall I play another?"

Miss Erstwhile: "What say you, Mr. Nobley? Ready to be done with me?"

"I think . . ." He bowed. "I think I will retire early. I bid you a good evening."

"And so ends the fun," Colonel Andrews said.

"Wait, I don't feel right . . . all that dancing . . ." Miss Charming put a hand to her forehead and fainted dead into his arms. He was forced to carry her to her chamber.

Clever girl, thought Jane, saluting her with two fingers. Touché, Miss Charming.

Boyfriend #7

Juan Inskeep, AGE TWENTY-FIVE

Gay.

day 9

AFTER BREAKFAST, THE GENTLEMEN WENT shooting, Aunt Saffronia was busy with the mute servants, and Miss Heartwright was still at the cottage, leaving Jane and Miss Charming alone in the morning room. They stared at the brown-flecked wallpaper.

"I'm so bored. This isn't what Mrs. Wattlesbrook promised me yesterday."

"We could play whist," Jane said. "Whist in the morning, whist in the evening, ain't we got fun?"

The wallpaper hadn't changed. Jane kept an eye on it all the same.

"I mean, is this what you expected?" asked Miss Charming.

Jane glanced at the lamp, wondering if Mrs. Wattlesbrook

had it bugged. "I am Jane Erstwhile, niece of Lady Templeton, visiting from America," she said robotically.

"Well, I can't take another minute. I'm going to go find that Miss Heartwreck and see what she thinks."

Jane's gaze jumped from wall to window, and she watched for hints of the men out in the fields, wondering if Captain East thought her pretty, if Colonel Andrews liked her better than Miss Charming.

Stop it, she told herself.

And then she thought about Mr. Nobley last night, his odd outburst, his insistence on dancing with her, and then his abrupt withdrawal after one dance. He truly was exasperating. But, she considered, he irritated in a very useful way. The dream of Mr. Darcy was tangling in the unpleasant reality of Mr. Nobley. As she gave herself pause to breathe in that idea, the truth felt as obliterating as her no Santa Claus discovery at age eight. *There is no Mr. Darcy.* Or more likely, *Mr. Darcy would actually be a boring, pompous pinhead.*

Wait a minute, why was she always so worried about the Austen gentlemen, anyway? What about the Austen heroine? Even poor Fanny Price leaned back, held her ground, and waited for her Edmond to come eventually to her. And Elizabeth Bennet—wonderful Elizabeth! Remember how quickly she learned her lesson after Wickham and laughed it off? Remember how easily she let the disappointment of Colonel Fitzwilliam slip off her shoulders? Jane was shocked to recognize in her old self more of the anxious, marriage-obsessed Mrs. Bennet than the lively Elizabeth. With her father's estate entailed away, marriage was not a convenience for Elizabeth—it was life and death. And even so, she managed to laugh and spin and wait to fall really in love. So. Jane couldn't give up men. Martin had proved that. But she could fling off her binding intensity, live out the dream now, and return to the world whole and Darcy-free.

She was ready to start right now. The morning room clock ticked. Nothing moved outside the window. She scratched her neck and sighed.

Chased by restlessness and anxious for action of any kind, Jane ran up to her bedroom to check her e-mail on her cell phone. Matilda barged in to clean, so Jane tucked her phone into her bodice and stole down to the library. From a seat near a window in the corner, she was hidden from the rest of the room and the sight line of the corridor. Stealth was her name, contraband electronic messages her game. It took her just a moment to scan her in-box for the one she wanted. Molly hadn't let her down.

Jane,

Couldn't turn up a thing on Martin Jasper of Sheffield, at least of our generation. Sorry. Clean living, maybe? Did search on Henry Jenkins of Brighton. No priors, no dependents. Studied theater and history at Cambridge. I read through transcripts of his divorce proceedings from four years ago—whoa, baby! Talk about melodrama. So, this Henry seems like a real rock, didn't let himself get baited by the barrister, but the stuff he recounts—his wife slept with the neighbor, he forgave her, she sold his car to pay for an impetuous weekend in Monaco, he forgave her, but when she shish-kebabbed his pet fish because he said he'd like to have children, he finally called it quits. Said stuff like he still loved the woman he married and always would. Then her testimony—she's the heartbroken, cast-off woman, but as soon as the other side starts in, she cracks, screaming like a banshee, and gets thrown out of court. Who is this guy that he stayed married to her for five years? You'll have to give me the scoop.

I miss you. I think it's great that you're there, I think you're very brave. Let's hit the coast after you get back. I'll lose Phil and the twins for the weekend, girls only. And if you run into Mr. Darcy, tell him I want my black nightie back.

XXXO,

Molls.

Jane was reading it for the fifth time when she heard voices on the other side of the bookcase. Her hands trembled as she turned off the phone, stashing it down her cleavage. When she calmed herself enough to listen, a man and woman's conversation echoed dully off the books.

"Miss Charming, I . . . I . . . that is—"

"Yes, Colonel Andrews?"

"Miss Charming, forgive my impudence, but I must speak with you alone or go mad. I have been wrestling with my feelings for some time and . . ."

Sounds of pacing.

"Yes, yes, go on."

"It is not easy, being the son of an earl. So much is expected of me, of the way I behave. I am known in town as a rake, a rogue, a rascal . . ."

Jane shook her head. Austen, she was sure, would not have written such dialogue.

"Is that so, Colonel Andrews?"

"Well, perhaps I was once, but I've grown tired of the act. I feel—deeply. I long to have someone who knows the true me, who I can be alone with and share my thoughts. And I have come to feel, with no uncertainty of the heart, that you are that someone. That someone is you, Miss Charming."

"Oh, Colonel Andrews!"

"My dear, dear Lizzy."

Giggling, sounds of smooching and whispers.

"You must tell no one—please, Lizzy. I am sworn to another, an odious widowed countess, but there must be a way out of the arrangement. I will find a way. I must have you, Lizzy. You are *enchanting*."

More giggling, some whispering, the sound of someone departing, and then Miss Charming's voice singing to herself, "Ha ha-ha ha ha-ha," before she wandered away.

Jane rested her forehead against the bookshelf and breathed out a very slow laugh.

Well, she thought, that proposal should be about as good a tonic to her fantasy as any.

Ah well. One gentleman down, two to go. The game was afoot.

Boyfriend #8

Bobby Winkle, AGE TWENTY-THREE

*Theirs was a relationship that began as friends and slowly trans-
formed, allure building like static electricity between their bodies.
They dated for six months during that between-undergrad-and-
grad-school, no-career-yet tricky time. Neither of their parents
made any fuss (he was black, she was white), and they just got
along so great, defying the hoot and holler of culture clash. He left
for an internship in Guatemala, a step toward his future career
in international affairs. They both cried at the airport.*

*He returned six months later and didn't call. Last year, Jane
heard that Bobby ("Robert" now) was running for Congress. At
a recent polling, he wasn't doing so hot in the thirty-something
jilted female demographic.*

days 9–10

WHEN THE MEN ENTERED THE drawing room before dinner, Miss Charming, who had been quietly slumped in her chair,

perked up and blushed, coy and self-conscious. Jane watched it play out—Miss Charming's need for acknowledgment of what had happened in the library, Colonel Andrew's stolen half smiles, Miss Heartwright's unaware melancholy. Strangely, Mr. Nobley (was he Henry Jenkins?) seemed in good spirits. For him. At least, he came into the room with almost a smile and kept something of it around his mouth all evening.

Jane grinned for Lizzy Charming through dinner. It was clear that forgoing the car and Florence was paying off. Then sometime around dessert, Jane felt a tick bite of jealousy. She scratched it away. It flared again, though this time it morphed into self-pity, but of the low-key, ladylike variety. The problem was that nagging, life-long question—What was the matter with her? Was she that unattractive? She'd never been really in love without having her heart mashed. And now, because she wasn't their typical client, would she be denied even fake love?

No. There were still two gentlemen left, and Miss Heartwright couldn't have them both.

"No more whist, I beg you," Aunt Saffronia said after dinner. "Let us have some music."

"Indeed," said Captain East. "I believe, Miss Erstwhile, that you promised me a song."

Jane was quite certain that she had never promised any such thing, but it seemed a fitting remark to make, and so Jane rose and made her graceful way to the piano.

"If you insist, Colonel Andrews, but I must beg you forgive me at the same time. And you too, Mr. Nobley, as I know you are particular to music played well and no doubt a harsh critic when a piece is ill executed."

"I believe," said Mr. Nobley, "that I have never been witness to a young lady about to play without her excusing her skill beforehand, only to perform perfectly thereafter. The excuse is no doubt intended as a prelude that sets up the song for deeper enjoyment."

"Then I pray I do not disappoint."

She smiled expressly at Captain East, who sat forward, forearms resting on knees, eager. With professional suavity, Jane arranged her skirt, spread out the music, poised her fingers, and then with one hand played the black keys, singing along with the notes, "Peter, Peter, pumpkin-eater, had a wife and couldn't keep her, put her in a pumpkin shell, and there he kept her very well."

She rose and curtsied to the room.

Captain East smiled broadly. Mr. Nobley coughed. (Laughed?) Jane sat back on the lounge and picked up her discarded volume of sixteenth-century poetry.

"That was . . ." said Aunt Saffronia to the silence.

"Well, I hope the weather's clear tomorrow," Miss Charming said in her brassiest accent. "How I've longed for a game of croquet, what-what."

THEY PLAYED CROQUET THE NEXT morning.

"Won't you show me how to use your mallet against the balls, Colonel Andrews?" asked Miss Charming, her eyebrows raised so high they twitched.

Colonel Andrews had trouble unplasticizing his smile.

Captain East chatted away the discomfort, his working-boy build meets gentleman grace working for him every inch. Not that Jane was looking at every inch, except when his back was turned. He kept the conversation on the weather, but did it in a very beguiling manner. To Jane's mind, clouds had never seemed so sexy.

As the game progressed, Andrews and Charming took the lead with professional zeal, followed by Heartwright and Nobley, an impressive pairing. Lingering in the rear, Erstwhile and East talked the talk but couldn't walk the walk. The worse they played, the more Jane felt inebriated on bad sports and her partner's undulating laugh. Captain East looked like he could play pro football, but he held the mallet in his hand as though being asked to eat steak with chopsticks, which Jane somehow found hilarious. He hammed it up for her benefit and made it very easy to laugh.

He straddled the ball and pulled the mallet back.

"Careful, careful," Jane said.

He swung—a hollow *thock*, and the ball smashed into a tree.

"I swear I'm trying my best." The captain's laugh made his voice go dry and deep, and Jane thought if he really let himself go, he might actually bray. "I've never played this game before."

"Captain East, do you see how Mr. Nobley keeps giving me that look?" Jane said, watching the couple ahead. "Do you suppose he's ashamed to know us?"

"No one could be ashamed to know you, Miss Erstwhile," said Captain East.

It was precisely the right thing to say, and somehow that made it wrong. Jane wondered if Mr. Nobley had heard it, wondered what he thought. Then asked herself why she cared. The only discovery she could make was a hard bite of truth, like a bite of apple stuck in her throat—she did care what Mr. Nobley thought of her. The thought rankled. Why was the judgment of the disapproving so valuable? Who said that their good opinions tended to be any more rational than those of generally pleasant people?

Jane's turn to swing. Her grip on the mallet slipped, the ball lurched forward a dramatic two inches, and they laughed again. Mr. Nobley was still staring their way. Was it possible that he wished he were laughing, too?

"Look, Miss Erstwhile," the captain said. "Someone is arriving." His voice twinged with interest, and she guessed the actor had no idea who it could be.

A carriage and two horses pulled up at the house's front. A new guest was big news at Pembrook Park, and all three couples abandoned the game to inquire. But soon they were able to see two servants carrying a trunk the wrong way—from the house to the carriage. Someone was going, not coming. And the trunk was Jane's.

When she spied Mrs. Wattlesbrook hovering about the scene, Jane felt her stomach squirm as though she smelled rotten meat.

"What's going on?" Jane asked.

"Your maid discovered an unmentionable among your things." Mrs. Wattlesbrook dangled a cell phone between her pinched fingers. Jane glared at the maid Matilda, who smiled smugly.

Probably gets a bonus for getting rid of me, Jane thought. The little turd.

"I believe I was very clear, Miss Erstwhile. We thank you for your stay and I regret that your actions have forced me to cut it short."

"You're really going to kick me out?"

"Yes, I *really* am." Mrs. Wattlesbrook folded her arms.

Jane bit her lip and bent her head back to look at the sky. Funny that it looked so far away. It felt as if it were pressing down on her head, shoving her into the dirt. What a mean bully of a sky.

Much of the household was present now. Miss Heartwright was huddled with the main actors, whispering, like rubberneckers shocked at a roadside accident but unable to look away. A couple of gardeners strolled up as well, tools in hand. Martin wiped his brow, confusion (sadness?) heavy on his face. Jane was embarrassed to see him, remembering how she'd ended things, and feeling less than appealing at the moment. The whole scene was rather Hester Prynne, and Jane imagined herself on a scaffold with a scarlet C for "cell phone" on her chest.

She realized she was still holding her croquet mallet and

wondered that no one felt threatened by her. She hefted it. Would it be fun to bash in a window? Nah. She handed it to Miss Charming.

"Go get 'em, Charming."

"Okay," Miss Charming said uncertainly.

"If you would be so kind as to step into the carriage," said Mrs. Wattlesbrook.

Curse the woman. Jane had just started to have such fun, too. Why didn't one of the gentlemen come forward to defend her? Wasn't that, like, their whole purpose of existence? She supposed they'd be fired if they did. The cowards.

She stood on the carriage's little step and turned to face the others. She'd never left a relationship with the last word, something poetic and timeless, triumphant amid her downfall. Oh, for a perfect line! She opened her mouth, hoping something just right would come to her, but Miss Heartwright spoke first.

"Mrs. Wattlesbrook! Oh dear, I have only now realized what transpired." She lifted the hem of her skirts and minced her way to the carriage. "Please wait, this is all my fault. Poor Miss Erstwhile was only doing me a favor. You see, the modern contraption was mine. I did not realize I had it until I arrived, and I was so distressed, Miss Erstwhile kindly offered to keep it for me among her own things where I would not have to look upon it."

Jane stood very still. She thought to wonder what instinct made her body rigid when shocked. Was she prey by nature? A rabbit afraid to move when a hawk wheels overhead? Mrs. Wattlesbrook had not moved either, not even to blink. A silent minute limped forward as everyone waited.

"I see," the proprietress said at last. She looked at Jane, at Miss Heartwright, then fumbled with the keys at her side. "Well, now, *ahem*, since it was an accident, I think we should forget it ever happened. I do hope, Miss Heartwright, that you will continue to honor us with your presence."

Ah, you old witch, Jane thought.

"Yes, of course, thank you." Miss Heartwright was in her best form, all proper feminine concern, artless and pleasant. Her eyes twinkled. They really did.

Everyone began to move off, nothing disturbing left to view. Jane caught a glimpse of Martin smiling, pleased, before he turned away.

"I'm so sorry, Jane. I do hope you will forgive me."

"Please don't mention it, Miss Heartwright."

"Amelia." She held Jane's hand to help her descend from the carriage. "You must call me Amelia now."

"Thank you, Amelia."

It was such a sisterly moment, Jane thought they might actually embrace.

They didn't.

Boyfriend #9

Kevin Hyde, AGE TWENTY-SEVEN

Man, Jane loved him. Sure, he wore an unnecessary tie to work and "weekend casual" meant khaki slacks, but who's perfect? She'd once made a list of "must-have attributes in future husband," and Kevin even made most of the "nice-to-have but not nonnegotiable" items. In retrospect, he'd had some kind of Darcy appeal about him from the very beginning, just in his mannerisms, his cool indifference, his falling for Jane despite the fact he hadn't wanted a serious girlfriend.

He played guitar, modestly. They did the Sunday crossword together. He loved his mom. He loved Jane. Until he told her over the blaring of a local car dealership ad that maybe he never really had.

"It's just gotten too hard, hasn't it? I mean, are you still having fun?"

Once in high school science, Jane's teacher had dipped an orange in liquid nitrogen and then thrown it on the floor, cracking it like glass. That's the only way she knew how to describe the physical sensation in her heart—cold and shattered. She tried to play it cool, to say, "Yeah, it's fizzling out, isn't it? Well,

let's still be friends." She tried, but she ended up pleading, her
nose running, making promises, splaying out her emotions in a
desperate way that would haunt her long after she'd forgotten
Kevin's smell.

They'd been together for twenty-three months. She'd gone
wedding-dress browsing on the sly. For a week, she curled up in
a corner, crying and consuming ice cream by the pint. At last,
Emma-esque, she burned Kevin mementos one by one in her
wok lid.

Frankly, it didn't help much more than the ice cream.

day 11

"REALLY, YOU MUST COME RIDING with us. I insist," Amelia
said, glowing even more than usual out in the autumn sun.

Mr. Nobley was wearing his pleasantly snug hunting breeches,
and though that *was* incentive, spending an afternoon as the third
wheel sounded beyond tiresome. But Jane was a tad curious to
watch the pair. She couldn't ask Amelia directly about Mr. Nobley
(for some reason, it seemed to be forbidden in Austenland—but really, in *Sense and Sensibility*, couldn't Elinor have asked her younger
sister if she was engaged to Mr. Willoughby? *That* silence had
seemed a touch extreme). So she spied for clues. Mr. Nobley never
touched Amelia, didn't so much as lean, step in closer, whisper in
her ear (or just breathe!), any of the subtle, Regency-approved PD
of A that Colonel Andrews gallantly drizzled over Miss Charming. Really, if Mr. Nobley had already declared his love for
Amelia, then he was a pathetic lover.

Or was he the kind of man who loved too much, who only
left his crazy wife because he wanted that much to be a father?

Wait, that wasn't Mr. Nobley, that was Henry Jenkins. But were they the same? It was all getting very confusing.

Jane tightened her bonnet ribbon, hoping it might help keep her thoughts snug in her head. She was certainly dressed for something rough in her pink morning dress (the bottom three inches stained from her surreptitious speed walks), with outdoorsy spencer jacket and her action bonnet, and had nothing to get her out of the ride, except maybe claiming a fake headache, but that was so cliché.

"Are you sure?" she asked.

Soon thereafter she was clambering into the ever-intimidating sidesaddle and whispering, "Easy, there, donkey friend," when Captain East appeared.

"Going for a ride, Miss Erstwhile?"

"Yes, and I wish you would come."

He had agreed before Amelia walked her horse into view. Captain East flinched but couldn't back out now.

Jane was determined to keep distant from the couple and have a little alone time with prince charming. Captain East didn't make her heart patter, but he was beyond high school quarterback cute, and being fake-courted by him would make for an interesting vacation at the very least. Then, like a bumbling fool, Mr. Nobley kept letting his horse trot forward, separating Jane and Captain East, and leaving Amelia riding alone. Jane would correct it, and Mr. Nobley would mess it all up again.

She glared. And still he didn't get it.

Then he was glaring, and she glared back the why-are-you-glaring-at-me glare, and his eyes were exasperated, and she was about to call him ridiculous, when he said, "Miss Erstwhile, you look flushed. Will you not rest for a moment? Do not trouble yourself, Captain East, you go on with Miss Heartwright and we will follow straightaway."

When the other two were out of hearing range, Jane turned her glare into words. "What are you doing? I'm just fine."

"Pardon, Miss Erstwhile, but I was trying to allow Captain East and Miss Heartwright a few moments alone. She confided in me about their troubled past, and I hoped time to talk would help ease the strain between them."

"Okay," Jane laughed, "so I'm a little slow." She knew she didn't sound the least bit Austen-y, but for some reason she just couldn't make herself try to approximate the dead dialect around Mr. Nobley.

After she swore herself to secrecy and did her best to seem trustworthy and closemouthed, Mr. Nobley revealed that those two had been more than fond acquaintances. In fact, last year he'd proposed and she'd accepted.

"Her mother disapproved, as he was merely a sailor. Mr. Heartwright, her brother, informed East that he was dismissed from being her suitor, and Miss Heartwright never had an opportunity to explain that it hadn't been her wish. She fears it is too late now, but I don't believe her heart ever let go of the man."

"Ah," Jane said, now fitting their story into the correct Austen novel context—*Persuasion*, more or less. And that was a real bummer. Captain East had offered Jane the best shot at curative love. Oh well. Two down . . . one to go? She studied Mr. Nobley and wondered why she had the impression that he was dangerous—or would be if he didn't so often look tired or bored. Was he a sleeping tiger? Or a sack of potatoes?

"And how do you feel about this, Mr. Nobley?" she asked.

"It does not matter how I feel about Miss Heartwright." He nudged his horse forward, and hers followed.

She hadn't been talking about Miss Heartwright, but, okay. "Wait, are you heartbroken?" She knew Miss Erstwhile shouldn't ask the question, but Jane couldn't help it.

"No, of course not."

"Not about Miss Heartwright, anyway." Jane watched Mr. Nobley's face closely for signs of Henry Jenkins. His mouth was still, unrevealing, but his eyes were sad. She'd never noticed before. "Maybe you're not heartbroken anymore, maybe you've passed that part, and now you're just lonely."

Mr. Nobley smiled, but with just half of his mouth. "You are very good at nettling me, Miss Erstwhile. As I said, it does not matter how I feel. We are speaking of Miss Heartwright and Captain East. I think it nonsense how they have kept silent about it these past days. They should speak their minds."

"You approve of speaking one's mind? So, do you approve of me?"

As it appeared Mr. Nobley had no intention of answering the question, and Jane was stumped at how to restart the conversation, they rode on in silence.

Of course just at that moment, she *would* see Martin by a line of trees, looking her way. Why couldn't she be chatting and laughing and having a wonderful time? She smiled generously at the world around her and hoped that Martin would think she was enthralled with Mr. Nobley's company and perfectly happy.

Mr. Nobley turned to ask her a question, but when he saw her grinning without apparent cause, the words hung in his mouth. His eyes widened. "What? You are laughing at me again. What have I done now?"

Jane did laugh. "I'm sorry, but I can't seem to help myself around you. You are so tease-able." Which was precisely not true, and yet saying it somehow made it so.

Mr. Nobley looked over his shoulder just as the line of trees hid Martin from view. Jane wasn't sure if he saw him.

"I'm sorry I annoy you so much," said Jane. "I'll stop. I really will."

"Hm," said Mr. Nobley as if he doubted it. He looked at his hands thoughtfully, not speaking again for several moments. In the silence, Jane became aware of her heart beating. Why was that? When he spoke again, his tone had changed, innocuous, chitchatty.

"How do you find Pembrook Park, Miss Erstwhile?"

"Do you mean the house itself? Well, it's beautiful, no question, friendly and yet too grand to be really comfortable. Like wearing a corset, I like how it looks and feels, but I can't relax in it." She shook her head. How did she keep slipping up? Saying things to this man that the Rules said she shouldn't. She tried to think of something more innocent to say. "I love the paintings. The ones hanging in the gallery, they're all in the grand style of portrait art, luminous with natural light. The artist isn't just concerned with outer beauty but takes pains to express the virtue of soul in the subjects and catch that gleam of importance in their eyes. I don't care how portly or drastically thin, how sickly or sad, all the people in those paintings know that they're significant. You have to envy that kind of self-assurance."

Jane stopped herself, realizing that she'd gotten carried away in the subject and her audience probably wasn't the least bit interested. A glance sideways at Mr. Nobley—he was watching her, intently.

"You're a painter."

Jane blinked. "I used to paint, but it's been years. Now I . . ." she paused, not knowing how to translate "graphic design" into Austen lingo. "It's been a while since I've used that medium."

"Do you miss it?"

"You know, I do, just lately. Maybe it's because my head's all mixed up," she nodded, acknowledging her awkward breakdown days ago, "but all the new things I'm seeing are bugging me, becoming images, and my hands twitch, wanting to work out those images on paper. I think drawing and painting used to be a way of thinking for me. Until I came here, I'd almost forgotten about it."

"Here I am!" Captain East was cantering his mount toward them. He rode beautifully, confidently. Molly's family spent their summers in the country, and she used to say that the way a man rides a horse could give you a pretty good idea how he would do something else. Jane eyed Mr. Nobley on his mount, noted that he was a smooth, gentle rider. The surprise of thinking this while wearing a bonnet made Jane choke. Her breath snarled in her throat, and she laughed.

Mr. Nobley's eyes widened. "What's funny? You often have some secret laugh, Miss Erstwhile."

"The way you have some secret displeasure?"

"No, not displeasure," he said, and she realized he was right. Sadness, or heartbreak, or grief that there was nothing to give him hope, perhaps. She was pretty sure now that he was Henry Jenkins, poor sop.

Captain East reined in beside Jane. "Miss Heartwright had a headache and went inside. So sorry to neglect you, Miss Erstwhile. You must tell me what I missed."

"I've discovered that Miss Erstwhile is an artist," Mr. Nobley said.

"Is that so?"

"It's been years since I picked up a paintbrush." She glared at Mr. Nobley, and *zing*, there was his smile again, brief, urgent. When his lips relaxed she wanted it to come back.

"That is a shame," said Captain East.

That evening when Jane retired from the drawing room, she found a large package on her side table wrapped in brown paper. She ripped open the paper and out tumbled neat little tubes of oil paints and three paintbrushes. She saw now that an easel waited by the window with two small canvases. She felt very Jane

Eyre as she smelled the paints and ticked her palm with the largest brush.

Who was her benefactor? It could be Captain East. Maybe he still liked her best, even after his tête-à-tête with Miss Heartwright. It could happen. Even so, she found herself hoping it was Mr. Nobley. Instinct urged her to stomp on the hope. She ignored it. She was firmly in Austenland now, she reminded herself, where hoping was allowed.

Did Austen herself feel this way? Was she hopeful? Jane wondered if the unmarried writer had lived inside Austenland with close to Jane's own sensibility—amused, horrified, but in very real danger of being swept away.

Ten days to go.

Boyfriend #10

Peter Sosa, AGE TWENTY-NINE

They met in the elevator. He worked on an upper floor, an ad exec, young for the position so obviously a genius. Smartness had always attracted Jane, that and hands and jawline and butt. And eyes. Also, integrity of character—she wasn't shallow. Peter fell for her at once, he said, because she was stunning. That's the word he'd used—stunning. It's a difficult word to dismiss. She longed to be that word to someone.

They went out every Friday night for five weeks, and she felt her heart plummeting a long way. Boyfriend #9 was still raw, a sore that wouldn't heal because she kept picking at it, but wouldn't Peter be such a way to come back from that catastrophe! She fantasized of the day she would casually bump into nasty ex-boyfriends with Peter on her arm. And then . . .

"What is it? You're married, aren't you?"

"No, no, nothing like that." He paused, leaving Jane to imagine. "I have a girlfriend. I'm sorry. I'm not cheating, she's right over there, at the table by the window. She made me a bet that I couldn't make the first girl I asked out fall in love with

*me. Some movie she saw, thought it would be romantic, then it
went too far . . ."*

Jane's language would have made Britney the longshoreman blush down to her boots.

days 12–13

THE NEXT MORNING, RAIN BLURRED the hard edges from
the world, transforming things into forms, like Christo's fabric-
wrapped bridges, nudes, and trees. Jane had been painting since
daybreak. Yellow, red, orange, blue. The colors made her hungry,
but she was too infatuated with paint on canvas to dress for breakfast. When Matilda came, Jane shooed her away.

She had forgotten the thrill she used to feel when buying a
new paintbrush, squeezing all those colors onto her palette, smelling
the clean natural odor of the oils, the reckless unknown of first
spoiling a white canvas. These past years, she had become comfortable with her mouse and computer screen, creating corporate art,
lazy and dull. And now, smearing green and gray together, inter-
rupting it with orange, she realized she had loved her last boyfriends
as a graphic designer would. But she wanted to love someone the
way she felt when painting—fearless, messy, vivid.

In honor of Miss Eyre, Jane did a self-portrait. When she
caught just the right shading of a cheek, her heart bumped her
ribs as though she were in love. What she was after was that self-
assurance in the eyes that those old portraits in the gallery had,
a knowing gleam that insisted she was worth looking at. It was
tricky to achieve. She wanted to ask someone else's opinion about
her painting, but not the traitor Matilda. Aunt Saffronia? No, she

was too eager to please. Martin? Oh, stop it. Mr. Nobley? Yes, but why him?

She made it downstairs late for lunch and a maid served her cold meats and well-cooked vegetables. The house echoed as though long deserted. She thought of returning to her easel, but she felt unsettled by the expression she'd left in her painting—she feared it was forced assurance, an actor's eyes. She decided to give both pairs of eyes a break.

She sat in the library, staring at the streaks of water against the window, the book *A Sentimental Journey* half open before her. What do gardeners do in the rain? she wondered.

Mr. Nobley had entered the room before he noticed her. He groaned.

"And here you are. Miss Erstwhile. You are infuriating and irritating, and yet I find myself looking for you. I would be grateful if you would send me away and make me swear to never return."

"You shouldn't have told me that's what you want, Mr. Nobley, because now you're not going to get it."

"Then I must stay?"

"Unless you want to risk me accusing you of ungentleman-like behavior at dinner, yes, I think you should stay. If I spend too much time alone today, I'm in real danger of doing a convincing impersonation of the madwoman in the attic."

He raised an eyebrow. "And how would that be different from—"

"Sit down, Mr. Nobley," she said.

He sat in a chair on the opposite side of a small table. The chair creaked as he settled himself. She didn't look at him, watching instead the rain on the window and the silvery shadows the wet light made of the room. She spent several moments in silence before she realized that it might be awkward, that conversation at such a time was obligatory. Now she could feel his gaze on her face and longed to crack the silence like the spine of a book, but she had nothing to say anymore. She'd lost all her thoughts in paint and rain.

"You are reading Sterne," he said at last. "May I?"

He gestured to the book, and she handed it to him. Jane was remembering a scene from the film of *Mansfield Park* when suitor Henry Crawford read to Frances O'Connor's character so sweetly, the sound created a passionate tension, the words themselves becoming his courtship. Jane glanced at Mr. Nobley's somber face, and away again as his eyes flicked from the page to her.

He began to read from the top. His voice was soft, melodious, strong, a man who could speak in a crowd and have people listen, but also a man who could persuade a child to sleep with a bedtime story.

"The man who first transplanted the grape of Burgundy to the Cape of Good Hope (observe he was a Dutchman) never dreamt of drinking the same wine at the Cape, the same grape produced upon the French mountains—he was too phlegmatic for that—but undoubtedly he expected to drink some sort of vinous liquor; but whether good, bad, or indifferent—he knew enough of this world to know, that it did not depend upon his choice . . ."

Mr. Nobley was trying very hard not to smile. His lips were tight; his voice scraped a couple of times. Jane laughed at him, and then he did smile. It gave her a little *thwack* of pleasure as though someone had flicked a finger against her heart.

"Not very, er . . ." he said.

"Interesting?"

"I imagine not."

"But you read it well," she said.

He raised his brows. "Did I? Well, that is something."

They sat in silence a few moments, chuckling intermittently.

Mr. Nobley began to read again suddenly, "*Mynheer* might possibly overset both in his new vineyard," having to stop to laugh again. Aunt Saffronia walked by and peered into the dim room as she passed, her presence reminding Jane that this tryst might be forbidden by the Rules. Mr. Nobley returned to himself.

"Excuse me," he said, rising. "I have trespassed on you long enough."

HE TRESPASSED ON HER AGAIN the following afternoon, and Jane found she did not mind whatsoever. Surprising twist, that. The rain had stopped, the sky bashful behind clouds, and at Mr. Nobley's suggestion, the party went walking the paths, avoiding the sodden lawns.

There was some fumbling of pairs, with Andrews and Charming at the lead, then the Nobley and Heartwright coupling turning into Erstwhile and Heartwright, which became Erstwhile and Nobley, and there the musical partners game ended. Jane glanced over her shoulder and wondered what thrills of pain and hope might be pricking Amelia as she walked with her erroneously jilted love. What fun.

"If it keeps raining all the time," Miss Charming was saying, "I'll go crazy. Can't we do something more than play cards and walk around?"

She squinted at Colonel Andrews to detect if he approved of her suggestion.

"Just so," he said, and Miss Charming beamed. "I've brought the very thing from London, a script from some little play or other called *Home by the Sea*. There are six parts, three pairs of lovers, just right for us, and it will give us something to pass the time before the ball, so let's rehearse and put it on for Lady Templeton."

"Oh, yes," said Miss Charming, clasping her hands at her chest, "jolly good, rather."

"I'll bet our Miss Erstwhile would be keen on it as well, right? Miss Heartwright would never disappoint me, I know, and East is a seafaring man—always ready for an adventure. What do *you* say, Nobley?"

Mr. Nobley did not answer immediately. "I think it inappropriate to stage a theatrical in the house of a respectable lady."

Miss Charming whined.

"Oh, come now, Nobley," the colonel said.

"I won't be entreated," he said.

Jane blew air through her lips like a horse. She'd liked the idea.

"Way to spoil it, Mr. Nobley," Miss Charming said. "Too bad Sir Templeton isn't here to play the third fellow. Will he be back soon, do you think, what-what?"

"I think not," Mr. Nobley said coolly.

"That's the pits. Hey Jane, what about that guy, I mean, bloke, I saw you talking to once in the garden? Do you think he'd play the part?"

Jane felt her toes go cold. "I don't know who you mean, Miss Charming."

"Sure you do, that tall bloke in the garden, one of the servants, maybe. I thought he looked pretty good standing next to you. He'd be better for your partner than Mr. Nobley."

"M-maybe it was one of the gardeners? I don't know." Jane peeked at Mr. Nobley's face. He was staring dead ahead, the shadows under his eyes making him look sleep deprived.

"Never mind," Miss Charming said, already bored with the idea.

The walkers tried various other topics on for size, but the Weather fit too loosely, Mr. Templeton's Disappearance was too short, and What Might Be for Dinner pinched a bit tight in the midsection. Then Colonel Andrews hit upon it—the fast-approaching Pembrook Park ball. They discussed the musicians that would be there, the guests arriving from other estates, the food, and the opportunity for romance. Miss Heartwright even put aside her melancholy to confer about gowns.

Jane's heart beat impatiently. A ball—things happen at a ball. Cinderella happened at a ball. Jane might happen. She felt hopelessly and wonderfully fanciful. The sun on her face, the bonnet ribbon under her chin, a wrap around her arms, and a hatted- and sideburned-man at her side, all lent itself to perfect suspension of disbelief.

She was so proud of herself! She really was diving into the world. Looking over Mr. Nobley, she wondered how this would end. It certainly was looking like East and Heartwright might kiss and make up, leaving Jane to Nobley. Or perhaps to no one. The puppet mistress Mrs. Wattlesbrook wouldn't go to any great lengths to ensure an engagement. And without his boss insisting on it, would Mr. Nobley even bother to woo her? It didn't seem likely.

Just ahead, the path was drenched in a puddle that could not be bypassed. The men walked through fearlessly. Colonel Andrews took Miss Charming's hand and helped her step across. Mr. Nobley placed his hands around Jane's waist and lifted her over. As he set her down, their bodies were much nearer than was seemly in the early nineteenth century. They held still for a breath, their faces close together. He smelled good enough to kiss. Her thoughts raged—I hate him and he hates me. It's perfect! Isn't it? Of course, he isn't real. Wait, am I supposed to be falling for someone or avoiding it? What was it again, Aunt Carolyn?

He was the first to step back. She turned away, and there was Martin. She'd forgotten Martin. Off and on, she realized now, she'd been forgetting the entire real world in order to let herself sink into the fantasy.

He was on his knees among some rosebushes. His face was shaded by his cap, but she could feel his eyes on her. As the party started to walk again, Martin rose and removed his cap as though the walkers were a funeral barge. None of the others seemed to notice his presence, and they disappeared into the full trees that leaned over the path.

Martin took a step forward. "Jane, can we talk?"

She realized that she was still standing there, staring at him, as though begging to be rejected again. She started to walk away. "Martin, no, I can't. They're waiting for me, they'll see."

"Then meet me later."

"No, I'm done playing around." She left him, that awkward line buzzing around her head like a pesky insect. And Jane thought, Done playing around, she says, as though she's not wearing a bonnet and bloomers.

Then she saw that Mr. Nobley had stopped to wait for her. His eyes were angry, but they weren't on her. She looked back. Martin had lowered his hat and thrust his hands back into the upturned earth.

Her heart was teeter-tottering precariously, and she almost put out her arms to balance herself. She didn't like to see them together, Martin, the luscious man who'd made her laugh and kept her standing on real earth, and Mr. Nobley, who had begun to make the fake world feel as comfortable as her own bed. She stood on the curve of the path, her feet hesitating where to go.

Then, the light became perfect.

After Jane's LASIK eye surgery, her perception of light had changed. In too bright light, she saw burned spots on her retina like one-celled creatures seen through a microscope; in high contrasts of bright and dark, both blurred together, the glow of car headlights bleeding into the night. But there was a certain kind of light that made the whole world 20/20—late afternoon when the sun is on a slant, pushing through the world instead of down on it. Just now, everything was distinct. Above her, all the leaves ringing like bells were individuals with cracks and curls, veins and prickly tips. Below, every blade of grass stood up in its own shadow, sharp and hotly green.

And she saw Mr. Nobley clearly. The thin wrinkles just beginning at the corners of his eyes, the whiskers on his chin darkening already after his morning shave, the hint of lines around his mouth that suggested he might smile more in real life. He had the kind of face you wanted to kiss—lips, forehead, cheeks, eyelids, everywhere except his chin. That you wanted to bite.

Jane thought: I wouldn't kick him out of bed for eating crackers.

Miss Erstwhile thought: My, what a catch. How the society page would rant!

"I think you should stay away from him, Miss Erstwhile." Mr. Nobley turned his back on Martin and took her arm, returning her to the path.

"I don't know why you care, sir," she said, doing her best to sound Austen-y, "but I certainly will, if you'll do me a favor. Perform in the theatrical."

"Miss Erstwhile . . ."

"Oh, come on! It will please me to no end to see you so uncomfortable. You're not afraid, are you? You seem so stuck on being proper all the time, but there can't be anything really wrong in doing a little theatrical. This is, after all, the nineteenth century. So perhaps your protests stem from your fear of appearing the fool?"

"You accuse me of vanity. It may be that the enterprise simply does not seem to me amusing. And yet in part you are right. I am not much of an actor."

"Aren't you?" She looked at him meaningfully.

He flinched and recovered. "My true concerns, however, are in regards to the delicate sentiments of our good hostess."

"And if we propose the recreation to her and she approves, will you participate?"

"Yes, I suppose I must." He tightened his lips, in annoyance or against a smile, she wasn't sure. "You are infuriatingly persistent, Miss Erstwhile."

"And you, Mr. Nobley, are annoyingly stubborn. Together we must be Impertinence and Inflexibility."

"That was clever."

"Was it? Thanks, it just came to me."

"No forethought?"

"Not a lick."

"Hm, impressive."

Jane jabbed him with her elbow.

When they caught up to the rest of the party, Miss Charming was engaging Colonel Andrews in a discussion on the "relative ickiness of tea" and Captain East and Amelia were either walking in silence or whispering their hearts' secrets.

"We're going to do the theatrical," Jane announced to the others. "Mr. Nobley is clay in my hands."

Boyfriend #11

Clark Barnyard, AGE TWENTY-THREE

Still not over boyfriend #9 and humiliated by #10, Jane declared she would shed her victimhood and become the elusive predator—fierce, independent, solitary! . . . except there was this guy at work, Clark. He'd make her laugh during company meetings, he'd share his fries with her at lunch, declaring that she needed fattening up. He was in layout at the magazine, and she'd go to his cubicle and sit on the edge of his desk, chatting for longer than made her manager comfortable. He was a few years younger than her, so it seemed innocent somehow. When he asked her out at last, despite the dark stickiness of foreboding, she didn't turn him down.

He cooked her dinner at his place and was goofy and tender, nuzzling her neck and making puppy noises. They started to kiss on the couch, and it was nice for approximately sixty seconds until his hand started hunting for her bra hooks. In the front. It was so not Mr. Darcy.

"Whoa, there, cowboy," she said, but he was "in the groove" and had to be told to stop three or four times before he finally pried his fingers off her breasts and stood up, rubbing his eyes.

"What's the problem, honey?" he asked, his voice stumbling on that last word.

She said he was moving too fast, and he said, then what in the hell had they been building up to over the past six months?

Jane sized up the situation to her own satisfaction: "You are no gentleman."

Then Clark summed up in his own special way: "Hasta la vista, baby."

days 14–18

AUNT SAFFRONIA, OF COURSE, DID not mind, and rehearsals began. It was a sentimental romance that even Jane in her present state of extreme open-mind/heartedness could not "ooh" at. But it made for several amusing days. She painted in the mornings and felt that artist instinct begin to yawn again inside her. In the afternoons she rehearsed with Mr. Nobley in the library, pacing outside under the apple trees (she didn't see Martin), or in the north drawing room with the others, wrapping themselves in fabric that was meant to suggest Roman togas.

And Mr. Nobley watched her. He had always watched her, of course. That was part of his *character*. But did she fancy that he did so even more now? And that in his side glances and half-smiles gleamed a touch of slipped-character, a break, a sliver of the man himself?

Jane's thoughts: Oh, stop it.

Jane's other thoughts: But then again, movie actors fall in love with each other on the set all the time. Is it so outlandish to suppose it might happen to me?

Jane answered Jane's other thoughts: Yes, it is. Stay focused. Have fun.

And, miraculously, she did! She bantered and laughed and smiled coyly over one shoulder. Her mornings painting imbued her with a fresh energy that made her feel pretty, and in the afternoons and evenings with Mr. Nobley, she felt relaxed. In the past, Jane would be so beset by stumbling doubts she'd lose the capacity to enjoy his eyes on her. But now, she looked at him right back. Here there was no anxiety, no what-ifs. Just good clean flirting.

One night as she snuggled into her sheets, giggling at herself and remembering all the delicious moments from that day, she decided that she was able to go for broke because she wasn't really Jane here—not obsessive, crazy Jane. Fairy-tale land was a safe place to roll around in, get into trouble, figure yourself out, and come out unscathed.

The night of the theatrical, Jane and Mr. Nobley secreted themselves behind the house for the final brush-up. The mood of late had let a bit of Bohemia into Regency England, the usual strict social observances bending, the rehearsals allowing the couples to slip away alone and enjoy the exhilarating intimacy of the unobserved.

Mr. Nobley sat on the gravel path, leaning back on his elbow in a reluctant recline. "Oh, to die here, alone and unloved . . ."

"That was pretty good," Jane said. "You genuinely sounded *in pain* as you said it, but I think you could add a groan or two."

Mr. Nobley groaned, though perhaps not as part of the theatrical.

"Perfect!" said Jane.

Mr. Nobley rested his head on his knee and laughed. "I cannot believe I let you railroad me into this. I have always avoided doing a theatrical."

"Oh, you don't seem that sorry. I mean, you certainly are *sorry*, just not *regretful* . . ."

"Just do your part, please, Miss Erstwhile."

"Oh, yes, of course, forgive me. I can't imagine why I'm taking so long, it's just that there's something so appealing about you there on the ground, at my feet—"

He tackled her. He actually leaped up, grabbed her around the waist, and pulled her to the ground. She screeched as she thudded down on top of him.

His hands stiffened. "Whoops," he said.

"You did not just do that."

He looked around for witnesses. "You are right, I did not just do that. But if I had, I was driven to it; no jury in the world would convict me. We had better keep rehearsing, someone might come by."

"I would, but you're still holding me." His hands were on her waist. They were gorgeous, thick-fingered, large. She liked them there.

"So they are," he said. Then he looked at her. He breathed in. His forehead tensed as if he were trying to think of words for his thoughts, as if he were engaged in some gorgeous inner battle that was provoked by how perfectly beautiful she was. (That last part was purely Jane's romantic speculation and can't be taken as literal.) Nevertheless, they were on the ground, touching, frozen, staring at each other, and even the trees were holding their breath.

"I—" Jane started to say, but Mr. Nobley shook his head.

He apologized and helped her to her feet, then plopped back onto the ground, as his character was still in the throes of death.

"Shall we resume?"

"Right, okay," she said, shaking gravel from her skirt, "we were near the end . . . Oh, Antonio!" She knelt carefully beside him to keep her skirt from wrinkling and patted his chest. "You are gravely wounded. And groaning so impressively! Let me hold you and you can die in my arms, because traditionally, death and unrequited love are a romantic pairing."

"Those aren't the lines," he said through his teeth, as though an actual audience might overhear their practice.

"They're better than. It's hardly Shakespeare."

"Right. So, your love revives my soul, my wounds heal . . . etcetera, etcetera, and I stand up and we exclaim our love dramatically. I cherish you more than farms love rain, than night loves the moon, and so on . . ."

He pulled her upright and they stood facing each other, her hands in his. Again with the held breaths, the locked gazes. Twice in a row. It was almost too much! And Jane wanted to stay in that moment with him so much, her belly ached with the desire.

"Your hands are cold," he said, looking at her fingers.

She waited. They had never practiced this part and the flimsy play gave no directions, such as, *Kiss the girl, you fool*. She leaned in a tiny bit. He warmed her hands.

"So . . ." she said.

"I suppose we know our scene, more or less," he said.

Was he going to kiss her? No, it seemed nobody ever kissed in Regency England. So what was happening? And what did it mean to fall in love in Austenland anyway? Jane stepped back, the weird anxiety of his nearness suddenly making her heart beat so hard it hurt.

"We should probably return. Curtain, or bedsheet, I should say, is in two hours."

"Right. Of course," he said, though he seemed a little sorry.

The evening had pulled down over them, laying chill like

morning dew on her arms, right through her clothes and into her bones. Though she was wearing her wool pelisse, she shivered as they walked back to the house. He gave her his jacket.

"This theatrical hasn't been as bad as you expected," Jane said.

"Not so bad. No worse than idle novel reading or croquet."

"You make any entertainment sound like taking cod liver oil."

"Maybe I am growing weary of this place." He hesitated, as though he'd said too much, which made Jane wonder if the real man had spoken. He cleared his throat. "Of the country, I mean. I will return to London soon for the season, and the renovations on my estate will be completed by summer. It will be good to be home, to feel something permanent. I tire of the guests who come and go in the country, their only goal to find some kind of amusement, their sentiments shallow. It wears on a person." He met her eyes. "I may not return to Pembrook Park. Will you?"

"No, I'm pretty sure I won't."

Another ending. Jane's chest tightened, and she surprised herself to identify the feeling as panic. It was already the night of the play. The ball was two days away. Her departure came in three. Not so soon! Clearly she was swimming much deeper in Austenland waters than she'd anticipated. And loving it. She was growing used to slippers and empire waists, she felt naked outside without a bonnet, during drawing room evenings her mouth felt natural exploring the kinds of words that Austen might've written. And when this man entered the room, she had more fun than she had in four years of college combined. It was all feeling . . . perfect.

"This is ridiculous," she said, then changed her mind. The last time she had confessed her real feelings to this man, it hadn't gone well. "Our lines, I mean, in this play. But I hope you will choose to enjoy it a little."

"Of course. It would be uncivil to say I will not enjoy making love to you tonight."

Jane's mouth was dry. "Wh-what?"

"Tonight as we perform the play," he said, completely composed. "My character professes love to your character, and to say that such a task is odious would be an insult to you."

"Ah," she said with a little laugh. "All right then." She had forgotten for a moment that "making love" did not mean to Austen what it meant today. Of course, Mr. Nobley the twenty-first-century actor knew that, and she squinted at him to see if he had been playing with her. He stopped walking, seeing something in the distance. She followed his gaze.

Captain East and Amelia were silhouetted by starlight. They stood in front of a bench, and he was holding both her hands.

"Are they acting?" asked Jane. "I mean, rehearsing for the theatrical?"

"They do not appear to be speaking at the moment."

He was right. They were completely occupied with staring into each other's eyes. Jane noted that Amelia seemed fluster-free for the first time since Captain East had arrived. If they were acting, they were doing a mighty fine job.

"You think it's real . . ." said Jane.

"It is not right to watch."

"If we don't watch, who will? Seems a shame to waste the moment with no audience to witness it."

Their lips moved now. Rehearsing lines? Or . . . Captain East leaned forward, Amelia tilted her head back. Her hand trembled on his chest. His lips met hers, briefly, gently. It clearly wasn't enough, and he seized her. She wrapped her arms around his neck, and their faces merged beyond distinction in the darkness. It looked pretty serious, the kind of affection those two might reserve for a sealing-of-the-engagement moment.

Suddenly, it wasn't like watching a movie—their passion seemed real and watching it started to feel like voyeurism. Jane wondered, Did Amelia the woman really love George East the man? The actor? Could she? What would happen to her heart when she left Pembrook Park?

"I'm in agreement with you now about the not-watching part," she said.

Jane and Mr. Nobley walked back to the house in silence, the air around them thick, dragging with awkwardness. Witnessing confessions of love and first kisses can be enchanting when you're with someone comfortable, someone you've already had that kiss with, and can laugh about it and feel cozy and remember your own first moment. Seeing it with Mr. Nobley was like having a naked-in-public dream.

"It's only natural to confuse truth and fantasy as they play parts in a theatrical," said Jane. "They start to feel as their characters would."

"True. Which is one reason why I was hesitant to engage in this frivolity. I do not think pretending something can make it real."

"I find it a little alarming that we agree on something. But do you think, in their case anyway, do you think those feelings could run deeper?"

Mr. Nobley stopped. He looked at her. "I wondered the same."

"I suppose it's possible."

"It's more than possible. They reside in compatible stations in life, they have like minds, their sentiments seem suited to each other."

"You sound like a textbook on matrimony. I'm talking about love, Mr. Nobley. Despite falling in love over a script, do you think they have a chance?"

Mr. Nobley frowned and rubbed his sideburns briskly with

the back of his fingers. "I . . . I knew Captain East in the past when he loved another woman. Her changes, her cruelty broke him. He was a shell for some time. If you had asked me last month if another woman's attentions could make him a whole man again, I would have said that no man can recover from such a wound, that he will never be able to trust a woman again, that romantic love is not air or water and one can live without it. But now . . ." He breathed out. He had not looked away from her. "Now I do not know. Now I almost begin to think, yes. Yes."

"Yes," she repeated. The moon hung in the sky just over his shoulder, peering as though listening in, breathless for what was next.

"Miss Erstwhile."

"Yes?"

He looked at the sky, he took several breaths as if trying to locate the right words, he briefly shut his eyes. "Miss Erstwhile, do you—"

Captain East and Miss Heartwright passed by, walking close without touching. Mr. Nobley watched them, his frown deepening, then he looked back over his shoulder at nothing.

What? What?! Jane wanted to yell.

"Shall we go inside?"

He offered his arm. She felt dumped-on-her-rear disappointment, but she took his arm and pretended she was just fine. Soon the warm safety of roof and walls cut off the luscious strangeness of night in the garden. Servants scurried, candles blazed, the preparations for the play were lively and unconcerned with a moment in the park.

Without another word, Mr. Nobley left her alone, his jacket still around her shoulders. It smelled like gardens.

* * *

TWO HOURS LATER, THE DRAWING room converted, the costumes wrapped, the electric-kerosene lamps flickering in a semicircle at their feet, the performers enacted the thirty-minute ode to love and the Mediterranean, *Home by the Sea*.

Miss Charming kept a ferocious grip on her script and gave oily air kisses to Colonel Andrews. Amelia was calm and sweet, melting into her dialogue with Captain East as though into his arms. Jane knelt beside Mr. Nobley, the wounded war captain, as he nearly died, and did her best to sound earnest. Old Jane would've run away or laughed self-consciously throughout. New Jane decided to feel as enchanting as Miss Charming and performed each line with relish and passion. It didn't matter that she wasn't a very good actress. Mr. Nobley's character miraculously recovered all the same, leading to the part where he stood and took her hands. They were still cold. He paused, as though trying to remember what came next.

He looked. Looked at her. At her and into her. Into her eyes as though he couldn't bear to look away. And there was a delicious curl in his smile.

"I love you," he said.

Zing, thought Jane.

It was his line, more or less, though simplified. Stripped of similes and farms and rain and moon and all, it pierced her. She opened her mouth to say her own line but couldn't remember a single word. And she didn't want to.

He leaned. She leaned.

Then Aunt Saffronia, who'd been laughing encouragingly during the parts that were supposed to be sad and clapping glee-fully whenever a new character came onstage, now cleared her throat as though intensely uncomfortable. Mr. Nobley hesitated, then kissed Jane's cheek. His lips were warm, his cheek slightly scratchy. She smiled and breathed him in.

At length, the six actors stood side by side, pretending the bright yellow wall of the drawing room opened to a view of the Mediterranean Sea, and said their closing lines.

Jane: *Trying to sound actress-y.* "At last, we are all truly happy."

Miss Charming: *Pause. Crinkling of paper. Frantic searching for line.* "Indeed."

Amelia: *With a shy smile for the tall man beside her.* "Our travels are ended."

Captain East: *With a manly smile for his lady.* "We can rest peacefully in each other's arms."

Colonel Andrews: *As always, with panache!* "And no matter where we may roam . . ."

Mr. Nobley: *A sigh.* "This will always be our home." *His voice unhappy with the line.* "By the sea."

And, silence as the audience waited for who knows what— a better ending line? A better play? Colonel Andrews cleared his throat, and Jane inclined her head in a hurried curtsy.

"Oh," Aunt Saffronia said and started the applause.

The audience clapped enthusiastically and arhythmically, and the cast bowed, Miss Charming giggling.

Jane squinted past the lamps to get her first good look at the audience, now that the play was over and stage fright couldn't prickle her. Aunt Saffronia, beaming. Mrs. Wattlesbrook, looking for all the world like a proud schoolmarm. Matilda, bored, and a few other servants, equally bored.

And Martin. He was in the back, and the room was dark, but no one else was that tall. Imagining the spectacle from his eyes, she saw anew how ridiculous that little play had been, and how all of Pembrook Park must seem so to him—the false lines, the feigned exclamations of love. Artifice. Pretense. Lies. Schoolgirl daydreams.

Jane leaned away from Mr. Nobley.

"Well, my dears, what a show. Quite professional!" Aunt Saffronia said, rushing their little stage. Mrs. Wattlesbrook was right behind her. A barrage of compliments engulfed the cast, and Jane smiled and nodded and smiled. She was conscious of Martin moving up, standing behind Mrs. Wattlesbrook, gesturing to Jane. Such a tall man was difficult to ignore. She ignored him.

"Uh, Miss Erstwhile?" he said quietly. He was shy. He was embarrassed. He sounded a little desperate.

Aunt Saffronia was plunging the profound intricacies of the script. Mrs. Wattlesbrook half-turned to glare at Martin.

"Miss Erstwhile?" he said again, sounding a little braver.

Jane met his gaze dead on. Martin blinked, smiled hopefully, and opened his mouth to speak again. What did he have to do with her? She was trying—for Carolyn, for herself, for her darling Mr. Darcy, she was trying to live this, and Martin's presence had the effect of shining a light on how shallow it all was, besides reminding her of every guy who had tossed her aside. She was having a grand time and his judgment was souring the punch. She turned her shoulder to him and addressed Mr. Nobley.

"Thank you, sir. Thus far the highlight of my stay has been making love to you."

Mr. Nobley bowed in acknowledgment. The conversation completely quieted. Jane thought she detected Martin sort of slump his shoulders.

"Well, good night, all," Jane said, and made a quick getaway to her room . . .

. . . where she lay on her bed, stared at her canopy, and wished that encounter didn't stick to her still, that she could just scrape it off her shoe. What would Martin have said if she'd let him speak? No, never mind, these things never end well.

Wait, there had been something good, coiling on the edge of her memory . . . ah yes, Mr. Nobley had been about to kiss her. She closed her eyes and held to that moment as she would to the tatters of a really great dream in the waking gray of dawn.

Tad Harrison, AGE THIRTY-FIVE

She'd broken down and purchased the Pride and Prejudice *DVDs by now (much to the lament of her video rental store's bottom line), but she hid them away for Tad's sake.*

Things got serious. They were engaged after a year, adopted a dog together, even picked out future baby names. But he wouldn't set a date.

"Things don't feel quite right," he'd say cryptically. "Not just yet. But soon."

After another year and some, she suggested they take a breather until things felt right, hoping that with a little distance he'd be ready to commit. She waited five months for him to make up his mind. He waited two weeks to start sleeping around.

The worst part? Worse than wasting over two years on that confirmed loser, worse than the humiliation of being cheated on? He got to keep the dog.

day 19

THE NEXT MORNING, JANE PAINTED in her chemise. She was satisfied with the self-portrait except for the eyes, which still looked back uncertainly. Since she'd only just taken up a brush again, she was not good enough to force the paint to do what it didn't want to do.

She meant to make it down for lunch, but she didn't have a timepiece and mislaid several hours tumbling through the second canvas, coming up for air again with a sprawl of the view from her window. She'd originally thought it would be lovely and pastoral, but it ended up very *Twilight Zone*, which she decided she liked even better. Somehow, it seemed more real.

She put down the brush, stretched, and realized that she was ravenous, so dressed, ate, and walked outside to hunt the gentlemen. With only two days left, her pulse clicked in her neck, Hurry, hurry! She was feeling at home here, no question. But what did she still have to do to feel resolved? How was she going to conquer Mr. Darcy?

No one was in the park. As she strolled by the servants' quarters, Jane stopped, guilt gnawing at her. Last night, Martin had called her name twice, and in front of Mrs. Wattlesbrook and everything. She should have at least given him the opportunity to speak.

Jane strolled casually to the servants' building and rapped on his door.

No answer. What a relief.

She rapped one more time and sauntered away, seeming not to wait. As she paced toward the end of the building, she overheard conversational tones. From behind the camouflage of a climbing rose vine, Jane peered around the side of the building and caught sight of Colonel Andrews smoking a cigarette and speaking to someone else just out of sight. The colonel was nodding and smiling, and seemed quite content. He passed the nearly defunct cigarette to the unseen person, who took a drag then flicked the butt away. Colonel Andrews checked his pocket watch and sighed.

"Well, time to get back to work." His smile vanished.

Probably has a meeting with Miss Charming, Jane thought.

She edged away from the servants' quarters and was ambling toward the front door when she heard someone overtake her.

"Ah, Miss Erstwhile," said Colonel Andrews. "I was just coming after you to join me in the stables."

"You were looking for me?" She waited for him to change his story. He didn't. "Uh, what about Miss Charming?"

"Miss Charming is resting in her chambers, but I cannot be idle. I must have some diversion."

"Are you sure she is? I mean, aren't you looking for her?" Jane felt a little dizzy.

"She told me of her plans after breakfast. You seem surprised that I was seeking you. Don't tell me that I've been so neglectful as to cause you this astonishment."

"Nap," she said. "Yes. I think I'll follow Miss Charming's example and rest myself. Perhaps, colonel, you need a break, too."

She left with a quiet swish of her skirt. *Back to work*. She was the work. *She* was. Rats. She'd had a sweet little hope that she was the treat, the rest from laboring conversations. Nope, hanging out with Miss Erstwhile was reason to sigh with exhaustion.

Did Mr. Nobley feel the same way? Could he have been the unseen smoker?

Tomorrow was the ball. She'd channeled all her hopes into the ball, where she would face the fantasy of Mr. Darcy and somehow . . . somehow just know what to do? She was all befuddled.

The ball had to be her closure, her triumph. But reminded that for these actor men, she was work, it was getting hard to keep her eye on the ball. She was not who she'd thought she was. No one was.

When she got back to her room, her self-portrait's eyes stared back, startled, even more unsure.

"Stupid art," she said.

Glum, glum, glum. That was the sound her feet made as she descended to the drawing room that evening. Glum, glum, as she walked alone at the back of the line of precedence into the dining room. It sure felt cold back there. She sniffed and rubbed her arms.

"Mr. and Mrs. Longley will be coming from Granger Hall and the two older Miss Longleys as well," Aunt Saffronia was saying, her conversation as endlessly full of names as the biblical lists of who-begot-whom. "Oh! And Mr. Bentley. Miss Heartwright, you recall Mr. Bentley? Still single and has four thousand pounds a year. Takes such good care of his mother."

Jane click-clacked her fork on her plate, pushing her food around. Her mother would've been shocked. It was not often that Jane was truly and absolutely despondent, and tonight she felt enslaved by that word. It shouldn't matter what they thought of her, she reminded herself. This was her game, and when she won it would be her victory. She just had to dig in her heels and keep playing. But the reality of the men being bored by her, paid to pretend to like her, intruded too much on her fun tonight, coupled with the dread that she wouldn't be able to conquer her obsession before her time in Austenland was up.

Jane tried to keep the despondency to herself, though Mr. Nobley seemed to be keeping a pretty good eye on her, as usual. She took another bite of . . . poultry of some sort? . . . and decided she'd pull the headache excuse out of the bag and dismiss herself to bed as soon as the dinner torture was over. She hated to waste a single moment of her last days, but she felt pulled inside out and couldn't figure out how to right herself.

She returned Mr. Nobley's gaze. His eyebrows raised, he leaned forward slightly, his mannerisms asking, "Are you all right?" She shrugged. He frowned.

When the women stood to leave the gentlemen to their port and tobacco, Mr. Nobley rose as well and made his unapologetic way to Jane's side.

"Miss Erstwhile, too long have you been asked to walk alone. May I accompany you to the drawing room?"

Her heart jigged.

"It's not proper," she whispered, the fear of Wattlesbrook in her. She didn't want to be sent home, not before the ball.

"Proper be damned," he said, low enough for just her ears.

Jane could feel all eyes on them. She took Mr. Nobley's arm and walked across that negligible distance, stately as a bride. He found her a seat on a far sofa and sat beside her, and except for the fact that she couldn't kick off her shoes and tuck her feet up under her, all felt pleasantly snug.

"How is the painting going?" he asked.

Of course it had been him (the paints). And of course it hadn't been him (Colonel Andrews's unseen smoking companion). Jane sighed happily.

"How do you do it? How do you make me feel so good? I don't like that you can affect me so much, and I find you much more annoying than ever. But what I mean is, thank you for the paints."

He wouldn't acknowledge the thanks and pressed her for details instead, so she told him how it felt to manipulate color again, real color, real paint, not pixels and RGBs, like the joy in her muscles stretching after a long plane ride. She talked about artists she admired, paintings she'd done when she was young and dramatic and how cowed by false emotion they seemed to her now, how the embarrassment of immature art had chased her away from the canvas for too long. And how grateful she felt, how chock-full of happy things just for having returned. She didn't worry that she was boring him, as Old Jane would've done. It didn't matter, she reminded herself. He was paid to listen to her and make her feel like the most interesting person in the world, and so, by George, she would be.

His lips pressed into a small smile that stayed. A very small smile. Sometimes almost imaginary. Jane wished that it might be bigger, that it might beam at her, but she supposed that wasn't the Nobley way. Then when she'd decided that his smile was a figment, Mr. Nobley said—or whispered, rather—

"Let's go look at your paintings."

What a delight, this man. How he kept surprising her, tossing aside his uptight propriety for her sake, murmuring plans for meeting in secret, fibbing to the others that he would withdraw early, then waiting upstairs for her to do the same. What a thrill to look around for watchers and scramble into her chamber, shutting the door behind them.

Jane stood with her back to the door, her hands still on the knob, breathing hard and trying to laugh quietly. He was leaning against the wall, smiling. The moment was giddily awkward as she waited to see what he had in mind, if he would suddenly shed Mr. Nobley and become some other man entirely. If he would break any other rules. The wait was agonizing. She realized she didn't know what she wanted him to do.

"I would love to see those paintings," he said, his voice still proper.

"Of course," she said. Of course he was still Mr. Nobley, of course the man, the actor, was not falling in love with her. And a relief it was, too, as she realized she wasn't ready to let go of Pembrook Park yet. Somehow she had to be by the day after tomorrow.

She presented the first painting, and he held it at arm's length for some time before saying, "This is you," though the portrayal was not photo-realistic.

"I couldn't quite get the eyes," she said.

"You got them just right." He didn't look away from the painting when he said, "They are beautiful."

Jane didn't know whether to thank him or clear her throat, so she did neither and instead handed him the second painting of her window and the tree.

"Ah," was all he said for some time. He glanced back and forth between both paintings. "I like this second one best. Beside it, the portrait looks stiff, as though you were too cautious, measuring everything, taking away the spontaneity. The fearlessness of this window scene is a better style for you. I think, Miss Erstwhile, that you do very well when you loosen up and let the color fly."

He was right, and it felt good to admit it. Her next painting would be better.

"I should let you retire." He held the self-portrait a minute longer, gazing at it as she had sometimes felt him look at her—unblinking, curious, even urgent.

She peeped through the keyhole to make sure no one was in the corridor before opening the door and letting him slip out. After a moment, she peered again and could see nothing, then Mr. Nobley's face dropped into view. He was crouching outside her door, looking back.

"Miss Erstwhile?" he whispered.

"Yes, Mr. Nobley?"

"Tomorrow evening, will you reserve for me the first two dances?"

"Yes, Mr. Nobley." She could hear how her voice was full of smile.

"Miss Erstwhile, may I come back in a moment?"

She yanked him back in and shut the door. Now he was going to grab her and kiss her and call her Jane, now she'd witness the pent-up passion that explodes behind Regency doors! But . . . he just stood with his back to the door and looked at her. And smiled in his way, the way that made her stare back and wish she could breathe.

"I should not put you in danger of Mrs. Wattlesbrook by staying," Mr. Nobley said, "but I suddenly had to see you again. I know that seems ridiculous, but I look at you, and I feel sure of something. Things are changing, aren't they?"

"Yes," she said, and they were, right at that moment.

He took her hand and looked at it a moment, then he turned it over. He lifted it to his mouth and kissed her palm.

"Tomorrow, then." And he left.

If only he was real! She stood and pressed her palm to her chest and breathed her pulse back into submission and thought she'd rather fancy a swoon.

To her self-portrait, Jane whispered, "This is the best therapy ever."

Guy after Boyfriend #12

Jake Zeiger, AGE THIRTY-ISH

One Saturday during the Tad era, Jane was checking the mail slot when Jake from 302 came up beside her. The nearness of their slots meant the back of his hand touched hers as he inserted the key.

"Hey, how's your dog?" he asked.

"Better. The vet said it was just something he ate."

"That's a relief, huh?" His smile was like a first kiss.

She stood there after he left, staring into the cavern of her mailbox, cold tingles passing through her body because she'd just had an Emma–loves–Mr. Knightley epiphany experience. She had just realized, "I might be secretly smitten with Jake."

She did not so much as whisper the idea to her houseplants. Then the week after it had become excruciatingly clear that she and Tad were over, Jane remembered Jake and let herself wish that tragedy might actually be opportunity. She walked down the hall to 302, hope bouncing in her step.

A bed-headed Jake opened the door, squinting.

"Hi, Jake! Hey, it's a beautiful day, and I was wondering, I noticed that you have Rollerblades, too, and I was wondering if you'd like to go to the park, with me, maybe after—"

"You woke me up for this? It's not even ten in the morning."

He rubbed his face and appeared to be heading back to bed as he shut the door.

day 20

JANE'S BALL GOWN WAS BRIDAL white. Lace and ruffles, tiny seashells beaded around bodice and hem, a low neck, and cap sleeves. She wore long gloves, her hair up with rosebuds, a string of pearls around her neck, and twenty-first-century makeup products. A maid other than Matilda helped her dress and do her hair, then stood back and said, "Oh, my."

It was very gratifying.

Jane surveyed the party from the top of the stairs, hoping to hear music before she descended. Gentlemen, most of whom she had never seen before, were in their fine black-and-white attire. Women swirled and laughed, all in white, coming and going between the drawing room and great hall, helping each other pin up their trains for the dance. It reminded Jane of the time she'd used the women's bathroom at the Mirage in Las Vegas, every inch of mirror jammed with brides in a hurry.

Some of the guests she recognized as servants and gardeners, dressed up for the night as local gentry. Others had that thin college undergrad look, the kind who donate plasma and volunteer for bizarre clinical studies to make a few extra bucks. Others seemed to be actors of the community-theater variety—slick and self-aware, overanimated, their ball gowns wafting a costume-closet scent of mothballs and cloves. But there were at least three women who had that Miss Charming jovial glint, that Miss Heartwright engaging earnestness, or that (did she dare admit it?) Miss Erstwhile bewildered hope. There were other Pembrook Parks, then. Sister estates. Some of the guests were actors, some players. Just who was real in this place, anyway?

Mr. Nobley was walking briskly from one room to the next, his eyes up as though trying to avoid eye contact. He looked scrumptious in his black jacket and white tie. Even better when he saw her and stopped. Really looked. *Zing.* Hello, Nobley.

"Mr. Nobley!" A stranger woman of retirement age waved a handkerchief gleefully and bustle-jogged toward him. Mr. Nobley fled.

And then, Martin was there, in tails, cravat, and all, and scanning the crowd.

For my face, she thought.

It was Martin's turn to look up, to see her. His expression was—whoa, she knew now that she was looking pretty good. Others noticed his expression and turned as well. The murmuring hushed and music swirled from the other room. She was Cinderella entering alone. What, no trumpets?

Martin rushed up several steps to escort her down.

"I'm fine," she whispered.

He took her arm anyway. "That's a crackin' dress, Jane. I mean . . . Miss Erstwhile. Might I have the pleasure of obtaining your hand for the next two dances?"

Ah, his smell! She was in his room again, static on the TV, a can of root beer so cold it was sweating, his hands touching her face. She wanted him close. She wanted to feel as real as she had those nights. Her sleeves pinched her shoulders, her dress felt heavy in the skirts.

"I can't, Martin," she said. "I already promised—"

"Miss Erstwhile." Mr. Nobley was standing at her elbow. He bowed civilly. "The first dance is beginning, if you care to accompany me."

Was there a look that passed between the two men? Some heated past? Or would they (wahoo!) have a jealous tussle over Jane's attentions?

Nope. Mr. Nobley led her away. Martin stayed put, watching her go, something of a puppy dog in his eyes. She tried to say with her own, "I'm sorry I ignored you the night of the theatrical and I understand why you judged me for being the kind of woman to fall in love with this fantasy and I'll be back and maybe we can talk then or just make out," though she didn't know how much of that she actually communicated. Maybe just a part, like "I'm sorry" or "you judged me" or "make out."

Jane and Mr. Nobley entered the great hall, the ceiling dazzling with thousands of real candles that put fire into the white dresses and cravats. Five musicians were seated on a dais—a cello and two violins (or maybe a viola?), a harpsichord, and some kind of wind instrument. From keys and strings, they coaxed a grand prelude to the minuet. Jane looked at everything, smiling at the amusement park novelty of it all. She looked at Mr. Nobley. He was beaming at her. At last.

"You are stunning," he said, and every inch of him seemed to swear that it was true.

"Oh," she said.

He kissed her gloved fingers. He was still smiling. There was something different about him tonight, and she couldn't place what it was. Some new plot twist, she presumed. She was eager to roll around in all the plot she could on her last night, though once or twice her eyes strayed to spot Martin.

Mr. Nobley stood opposite her in a line of ten men. She

watched Amelia and Captain East perform the figures. They held each other's gazes, they smiled with the elation of new love. All very convincing.

Poor Amelia, thought Jane.

It was a bit cruel, now that she thought about it, all these actors who made women fall in love with them. Amelia seemed so tenderhearted, and Miss Charming and her heaving breasts so delighted with this world. Jane caught sight of a very striking Colonel Andrews who, now that she watched him dance, might just be gay.

Jane felt a thrumming of foreboding. All the ladies were so happy and open-hearted and eager to love. What would happen to them in the dregs of tomorrow?

Two pairs of strangers performed. Jane watched them. Mr. Nobley watched her. Then it was her turn.

She curtsied to the audience, to Mr. Nobley, and faced him in the center of the floor. All eyes watched them. Jane looked for Martin in the crowd.

Maybe I really don't want this, she thought. This is summer camp. This is a novel. This isn't home. I need something real. Root beer and disposable umbrellas and bare feet real.

"I believe we must say something."

It was Mr. Nobley who spoke.

"Sorry," she said.

"Are you unwell tonight?"

"Do I look unwell?"

He smiled. "You are baiting me. It will not work tonight, Miss Erstwhile. I am completely at ease. I might even say, I am quite content."

Jane pushed the air out of her lungs. Part of her very much wanted to banter and play, to twirl and laugh, to be Miss Erstwhile and fall in love with Mr. Nobley (fall back in love?), but she felt herself on that razor's edge, walking toe to heel like a gymnast, and when she fell this time, she wanted to be on the real world side, away from heartless fantasy, into the tangible.

Then, with his hand on her waist to lead her through another figure, Mr. Nobley smiled at her again, and she clean forgot what she wanted.

Him, him, him! she thought. I want him and this and everything, every flower, every strain of music. And I don't want it wrapped up in a box—I want it living, around me, real. Why can't I have that? I'm not ready to give it up.

The first number ended, the group applauded the musicians. Mr. Nobley seemed to applaud Jane.

"You look flushed," he said. "I will get you a drink."

And he was gone.

Jane smiled at his back. She liked a man in tails. Something bumped her elbow.

"Excuse me . . . oh, it is you, Jane, dear," said Aunt Saffronia. She'd been watching Mr. Nobley as well, and her expression was still misty with contemplation. "Where is your partner off to?"

"He is fetching me a drink," said Jane. "I've never seen him so attentive. Or so at ease."

"Nor I, not in the four years I have known him. He is acting like a proper gentleman in love, is he not? I might almost say that he looks happy." Aunt Saffronia was thoughtful, and while she stared, she idly bit her fingernail right through her glove.

"Is he in love?" asked Jane. She was feeling bold in her bridal gown.

"Hm, a question only hearts can answer." She looked fully at Jane now and smiled approvingly. "Well, you are a confection tonight! And no wonder."

Aunt Saffronia leaned in to touch cheeks and kiss, and Jane caught a trace of cigarette smoke. Could the dear lady be the unseen smoker? What a lot of secrets in this place, thought Jane. She'd never before considered that Austen didn't just write romances and comedies, but mysteries as well.

Mr. Nobley walked briskly to her side, offering a cup from the punch bowl, asking her if she required anything else while she drank.

"Is it too hot in here for you? I will have them open the windows. Or I could fetch you a fan."

"No, I'm fine, sir."

He was impatient for a servant to come take her empty cup and glared at anyone who interrupted their path back to the dance floor.

"You're not enjoying the ball?" she asked.

"I assure you, I am taking an inordinate amount of pleasure from this ball, but none of it has to do with any of these bumblers."

"I think you just complimented me," said Jane. "You should take better care next time."

The music had started, the couples had begun a promenade, but Mr. Nobley paused to hold Jane's arm and whisper, "Jane Erstwhile, if I never had to speak with another human being but you, I would die a happy man. I would that these people, the music, the food and foolishness all disappeared and left us alone. I would never tire of looking at you or listening to you." He took a breath. "There. That compliment was on purpose. I swear I will never idly compliment you again."

Jane's mouth was dry. All she could think to say was, "But . . . but surely you wouldn't banish *all* the food."

He considered, then nodded once. "Right. We will keep the food. We will have a picnic."

And he spun her into the middle of the dance. While the music played, they didn't speak again. All his attention was on her, leading her through the motions, watching her with admiration.

He danced with her as though they were evenly matched, no indication that she was the lone rider of the Precedence Caboose. She had never before felt so keenly that Mr. Nobley and Miss Erstwhile were a couple.

But I'm not really Miss Erstwhile, thought Jane.

Her heart was pinching her. She needed to get away, she was dizzy, she was hot, his eyes were arresting, he was too much to take in.

What am I supposed to do, Aunt Carolyn? she asked the ceiling. Everything's headed for Worse Than Before. How do I get out of this alive?

She spun and saw Martin, and kept her eyes on him as though he were the lone landmark in a complicated maze. Mr. Nobley noticed her attention skidding. His eyes were dark when he saw Martin. His recent smile turned down, his look became more intense.

As soon as the second number ended, Jane curtsied, thanked her partner, and began to depart, anxious for a breath of cold November air.

"A moment, Miss Erstwhile," Mr. Nobley said. "I have already taken your hand for the last half hour, but now I would beg your ear. Might we . . ."

"Mr. Nobley!" A woman with curls shaking around her face flurried his way. Had Mr. Nobley been making visits to other estates while he was supposed to be hunting? Or was this a repeat client who might've known the man from a past cast? "I'm so happy to find you! I insist on dancing every dance."

"Just now is not . . ."

Jane took advantage of the interruption to slip away, searching above the tops of heads for Martin. He'd been just over there . . . a hand grabbed her arm.

She turned right into Mr. Nobley, their faces close, and she was startled by the wildness in him now, a touch of Heathcliff in his eyes. "Miss Erstwhile, I beg you."

"Oh, Mr. Nobley!" said another lady behind him.

He glanced back with a harried look and gripped Jane's arm tighter. He walked her out of the ballroom and into the darkened library, only then releasing her arm, though he had the good grace to look embarrassed.

"I apologize," he said.

"I guess you would."

He was blocking the escape, so she gave in and took a chair. He began to pace, rubbing his chin and occasionally daring to look at her. The candlelight from the hallway made of him a silhouette, the starlight from the window just touching his eyes, his mouth. It was as dark as a bedroom.

"You see how agitated I am," he said.

She waited, and her heart set to thumping without her permission.

He wildly combed his hair with his fingers. "I can't bear to be out there with you right now, all those indifferent people watching you, admiring you, but not really caring. Not as I do."

Jane: (hopeful) Really?

Jane: (practical) Oh, stop that.

Mr. Nobley sat in the chair beside her and gripped its arm.

Jane: (observant) This man is all about arm gripping.

"Well do I remember the first night we met, how you questioned my opinion that first impressions are perfect. You were right to do so, of course, but even then I suspected what I've come to believe most passionately these past weeks: from that first moment, I knew you were a dangerous woman, and I was in great peril of falling in love."

She thought she should say something witty here.

She said, "Really?"

"I know it seems absurd. At first, you and I were the last match possible. I cannot name the moment when my feelings altered. I recall a stab of pain the afternoon we played croquet, seeing you with Captain East, wishing like a jealous fool that I could be the man you would laugh with. Seeing you tonight . . . how you look . . . your eyes . . . my wits are scattered by your beauty and I cannot hide my feelings any longer. I feel little hope that you have come to feel as I do now, but hope I must."

He placed his gloved hand on top of hers, as he had in the park her second day. It seemed years ago.

"You alone have the power to save me this suffering. I desire nothing more than to call you Jane and be the man always by your side." His voice was dry, cracking with earnestness. "Please tell me if I have any hope."

After a few moments of silence, he popped back out of his chair again. His imitation of a lovesick man in agony was very well done and quite appealing. Jane was mesmerized. Mr. Nobley began to test the length of the room again. When his pacing reached a climax, he stopped to stare at her with clenched desperation. "Your reserve is a knife. Can you not tell me, Miss Erstwhile, if you love me in return?"

Oh, perfect, perfect moment.

But even as her heart pounded, she felt a sense of loss, sand so fine she couldn't keep it from pouring through her fingers. Mr. Nobley *was* perfect, but he was just a game. It all was. Even Martin's meaningless kisses were preferable to the phony perfection. She was craving anything real—bad smells and stupid men, missed trains and tedious jobs. But she remembered that mixed up in the ugly parts of reality were also those true moments of grace—peaches in September, honest laughter, perfect light. Real men. She was ready to embrace it now. She was in control. Things were going to be good.

She stared at the hallway and thought of Martin. He'd been the first real man in a long time who'd made her feel pretty again, whom she'd allowed herself to fall for. And not the Jane-patented-oft-failed-all-or-nothing-heartbreak-love, but just the sky-blue-lean-back-happy-calm-giddy-infatuation. She looked at Mr. Nobley and back at the hallway, feeling like a pillow pulled in two, her stuffing coming out.

"I don't know. I want to, I really do . . ." She was replaying his proposal in her mind—the emotion behind it had felt skin-tingling real, but the words had sounded scripted, secondhand, previously worn. He was so delicious, the way he looked at her, the fun of their conversations, the simple rapture of the touch of his hand. But . . . but he was an actor. She would have liked to play into this moment, to live it wholeheartedly in order to put it behind her. An unease stopped her.

The silence stretched, and she could hear him shift his feet. The lower tones of the dancing music trembled through the walls, muffled and sad, stripped of vigor and all high prancing notes.

Surreal, Jane thought. That's what you call this.

"Miss Erstwhile, let me impress upon you my utmost sincerity . . ."

"There's no need." She sat up straighter, smoothed her hands over her skirt. "I understand completely. But I guess I just can't. I can't do it anymore. I did my best, and this place was really good for me, you were really good for me. But I've come to the end. And it's okay."

Something in her tone must have caught at him. He knelt beside her, taking her hand. "Are you? Are you okay?" he asked in more honest, feeling tones than she had ever heard from him.

The change startled her. Despite his austere looks, he had an openness about his expression that she could only account for in his eyes. Dark eyes, focused on her, pleading with her. But it was all just a game.

"I don't know you," she said softly.

He blinked twice. He looked down. "Perhaps I spoke too soon. Forgive me. We can speak of this later." He rose to leave.

"Mr. Nobley," she said, and he stopped. "Thank you for thinking kindly of me. I can't accept your proposal, and I won't ever be able to. I'm flattered by your attentions, and I have no doubt that many a fine lady will melt under such proclamations in the future."

"But not you." He sounded beautifully sad.

What an actor, she thought.

"No, I guess not. I'm embarrassed that I came here at all as though begging for your tormented, lovesick proposal. Thank you for giving it to me so that I could see that it's not what I want."

"What do you want?" His voice nearly growled with the question.

"Excuse me?"

"I am asking sincerely," he said, though he still sounded angry. "What do you want?"

"Something real."

He frowned. "Does this have anything to do with a certain gardener?"

"Don't argue with me about this. It's none of your business."

He scowled but said, "I truly wish you every happiness, Miss Erstwhile, whom I will never call Jane."

"Let's toss the pretense out the window, shall we? Go ahead and call me Jane." He seemed saddened by that invitation, and she remembered what it meant to a Regency man to call a woman by her first name. "Except it won't imply that we're engaged or anything . . . Never mind. I'm sorry, I feel like a fool."

"I am the fool," he said.

"Then here's to fools." Jane smiled sadly. "I should return."

Mr. Nobley bowed. "Enjoy the ball."

She left him in the dark library, startling herself with the suddenness of yet another ending. But she'd done it. She'd said no. To Mr. Nobley, to the idea of Mr. Darcy, to everything that held her back. She felt so light, her heels barely touched the floor.

I'm done, Carolyn, I know what I want, she thought as she approached the palpable strokes of dancing music.

A HAND TOUCHED HER SHOULDER. "Miss Erstwhile," Martin said.

Jane spun around, guilty to have just come from a marriage proposal, ecstatic at her refusal, dispirited by another ending, and surprised to discover Martin was the one person in the world she most wanted to see.

"Good evening, Theodore," she said.

"I'm Mr. Bentley now, a man of land and status, hence the fancy garb. They'll allow me to be gentry tonight because they need the extra bodies, but only so long as I don't talk too much."

His eyes flicked to a point across the room. Jane followed his glance and saw Mrs. Wattlesbrook wrapped in yards of lace and eyeing them suspiciously.

"Let's not talk, then." Jane pulled him into the next dance.

He stood opposite her, tall and handsome and so real there among all the half-people.

They didn't talk as they paraded and turned and touched hands, wove and skipped and do-si-doed, but they smiled enough to feel silly, their eyes full of a secret joke, their hands reluctant to let go. As the dance finished, Jane noticed Mrs. Wattlesbrook making her determined way toward them.

"We should probably . . ." Martin said.

Jane grabbed his hand and ran, fleeing to the rhythm of another dance tune, out the ballroom door and into a side corridor. Behind them, hurried boot heels echoed.

They ran through the house and out back, crunching gravel under their feet, making for the dark line of trees around the perimeter of the park. Jane hesitated before the damp grass.

"My dress," she said.

Martin threw her over his shoulder, her legs hanging down his front. He ran. Jostled on her stomach, Jane gave out laughter that sounded like hiccups. He weaved his way around hedges and monuments, finally stopping on a dry patch of ground hidden by trees.

"Here you are, my lady," he said, placing her back on her feet. Jane wobbled for a moment before gaining her balance.

"So, these are your lands, Mr. Bentley."

"Why, yes. I shape the shrubs myself. Gardeners these days aren't worth a damn."

"I should be engaged to Mr. Nobley tonight. You know you've absolutely ruined this entire experience for me."

"I'm sorry, but I warned you, five minutes with me and you'll never go back."

"You're right about that. I'd decided to give up on men entirely, but you made that impossible."

"Listen, I'm not trying to start anything serious. I just—"

"Don't worry." Jane smiled innocently. "Weird intense Jane gone, new relaxed Jane just happy to see you."

"You do seem different." He touched her arms, pulled her in closer. "I'm happy to see you too, if you'd know. I think I missed you a bit."

"That's the nicest thing you've ever said to me."

"I'm certain I could think of something nicer." He looked up, thinking before turning back to her again. "I'm sorry about what I said before. All the other women I've seen at Pembrook

Park seemed to be toying with ideas of affairs while their husbands were on business trips. I couldn't reconcile what I knew of the women who come here and what I knew of you. When I saw you that day walking with Mr. Nobley and the others, I realized you're here because you're not satisfied—you're looking for something. And when I finally realized that, can you imagine how lucky I felt that out of everyone, you would choose me?"

"Thanks," she said. "That was honest and encouraging, but Martin, you were going for *nice*."

"I wasn't finished yet! I also wanted to tell you that you're beautiful."

"That's better."

"Unbelievably beautiful. And . . . and I don't know how to say it. I'm not very good at saying what I'm thinking. But you make me feel like myself." He swept a loose lock of hair from her forehead. "You remind me of my sister."

"Oh, really? You have *that* kind of sister?"

"Yes, confident, funny . . ."

"No, I meant the kind that you want to smooch."

Martin swept her up again, this time in a more romantic style than the over-the-shoulder baggage. She fit her arm around his neck and let him kiss her.

She pressed her hand to his chest, trying to detect if his heart was pounding like hers. She peered at him and saw a little frown line between his eyes.

"No, my sister doesn't kiss half so well."

He walked her around, singing some ludicrous lullaby as though she were a baby, then set her down on a tree stump so they were nearly the same height.

"Martin, could you lose your job over this?"

He traced the line of her cheek with his finger. "At the moment, I don't care."

"I'll talk to Mrs. Wattlesbrook about it at our departure meeting tomorrow, but I don't think my opinion means much to her."

"It might. Thank you."

Then there was silence and with it a hint of ending, and Jane realized she wasn't quite ready for it. Martin was the first real guy she'd ever been able to relax with, turn off the obsessive craziness and just have fun. She needed to be with him longer and practice up for the real world.

"I'm supposed to leave tomorrow," she said, "but I can stay a couple more days, change my flight. I could find a hotel in London, far away from Wattlesbrook's scope of vision, and I could see you. Just hang out a bit before I go home, no weirdness, no pressure, I promise."

He smiled broadly. "That's an offer I can't refuse because I'm simply mad to see you in pants. I have a feeling you have a very nice bum."

Boyfriend #13

Jimmy Rimer, AGE THIRTY-EIGHT

Jane had lost most of her social life with the departure of boyfriend #12 and the dog, so pretty much she stayed at home. Every night. Unless she worked late. Oh, joy.

A year hobbled by and Jane was still avoiding eye contact with the opposite sex. Molly tried to set her up with friends of Phillip's, but Jane blindly spurned them all.

Then, Jimmy. They walked the same path through Central Park every day, and despite her iron-willed reluctance, the romance just happened. It felt like a tiny, perfect miracle that she was allowing herself a chance to fall in love again. They decided not to burden each other with psychiatric profiles or travelogues through past failed relationships and instead just experienced each other. So refreshing! Such a graceful way to begin loving! For five months, Jane wondered why she'd never tried this before.

Then one fateful spring morning, Jimmy snorted while laughing. What's wrong with that? Absolutely nothing. It should be a cute idiosyncrasy in the man you adore. But it stung Jane like a hornet, and it swelled and itched and bothered her till she sat up in bed at two A.M. and thought aloud, Mr. Darcy would never snort.

She altered her route through the park.

day 21

JANE DIDN'T MAKE IT DOWN to breakfast that morning. She packed casually, wistfully, refusing the help of her maid, plopping her well-used hairpiece into the trash.

She looked out the window a lot. Then she twisted a decorative strip of metal from the lamp beside her bed and used it to carve *Catherine Heathcliff* to the underside of the windowsill. After hanging her self-portrait in the bathroom, she went back to the windowsill, adding the words *and Jane*.

When she tromped downstairs at last, she found the entire house had a sad, sleepy air of after-party. The ballroom was quiet and cold, the floor stained with tread marks, sticky pools of spilled punch in the corners. In the morning room, greasy and crumb-stuck breakfast dishes were abandoned on the table, cold meats and collapsing sweet breads sat on the sideboard.

Colonel Andrews was alone in the drawing room, reading. She didn't disturb him. Captain East and Miss Heartwright were taking a good-bye stroll through the park. Jane thought if she strolled that park one more time, it would permanently damage the sane part of her brain.

She passed Miss Charming in the corridor.

"Off you go, then," Miss Charming said. "Cheerios. I'm staying an extra day to get an eyeball of the new recruits and make sure they know my colonel is taken."

Jane air-kissed her cheek. "This is farewell, then, Lizzy, sister of my bosom."

"They're real, you know." Miss Charming placed her hands beneath her breasts and gave them a hearty shaking.

"Really?" Jane said, gaping openly.

"Oh, yes, real as steel. People always ask, so I thought I'd save you the wondering. As a parting gift."

"Thank you," Jane said, and she meant it sincerely. It was good to know what was real.

They said their good-byes, and on her way out, Jane passed by the library. There in a corner sat Inflexibility. He raised his eyes when he heard her footfalls.

"Oh," said Jane, antsy with embarrassment. "Good morning, Mr. Nobley."

"You weren't at breakfast," he said.

"I'm off." She indicated her bonnet and spencer jacket. "Just saying good-bye to the house. It's a lovely old house."

"New, actually. Built in 1809."

"Right." His insistence on maintaining the charade chafed her. She had a surging and ridiculous desire to plop down beside him and shake him and make him talk to her like a real person.

"Well, since I ran into you, I can thank you in person for a great vacation. I feel sort of sheepish that it didn't turn out differently."

Mr. Nobley shrugged, and she was surprised to detect anger in his eyes. Still playing the jilted man? Or had she wounded his actor's ego? Maybe he was denied a paycheck bonus for not getting engaged.

"It has been a pleasure to have you here, Miss Erstwhile. I might miss you, actually."

"Really?"

"It is possible."

"Hey, I've been wondering something . . . What is Mr. Nobley's first name?"

"William. You know, you are the first person to ask."

Any further awkwardness was cut off by the sound of an approaching carriage. Jane stepped out the front door for the last time, and she and Amelia, gratefully and mournfully, took their leave. Aunt Saffronia stood by the door, waving her handkerchief and shedding rather impressive tears. Colonel Andrews strolled out to wave good-bye with the stately line of house servants in their white caps and white wigs. Captain East smiled knowingly, his eyes earnest with whatever fake promises he and Amelia had made. Mr. Nobley didn't bother to join the farewell.

Jane looked for Martin, but he was absent. No matter. After the driver left her at Heathrow, she was to change her ticket and meet him at a certain pub.

As their carriage pulled away, two men Jane had never seen before emerged from the house—one young and handsome enough to be fresh meat for the new girls, and the other a portly, red-faced gentleman who looked mildly sloshed. The new Sir Templeton, she realized, and felt oddly delighted that without her the story would still go on.

Amelia cast off her bonnet, leaned back, and snuggled against Jane's arm.

"What a time!" she said in an American accent. "The best so far."

"You're not British?"

"No, no, but after my first visit here—this is my fourth—I got myself some private drama tutoring. My first character was scatterbrained and immature, and my drama coach helped me refine my Austenian self and get the accent down. It makes all the difference. If you live in the Bay Area, I could hook you up with my coach. He's divine."

"No, that's okay, I won't be coming back."

"Not come back? Your husband put up a squeal about the price, did he? Well, you just steamroll over his protests. Those men want pretty wives but aren't willing to put up the cash to make us happy. Tell him to talk to my therapist if he needs convincing. Or my lawyer. I'll give you their cards."

Jane shifted a bit to her right, feeling as though she were cuddled up to a stranger. She noticed for the first time Amelia's roots dark with three weeks' growth. "Actually, I'm not—"

"Did you see my face when Captain East first arrived? What a thrill! Honestly, I didn't know that they'd bring back the same actor for me. This year I asked to stay in the cottage because last year the other women at the big house were so annoying, but I was getting bored until George showed up. Uhh, he's such a *hunk*. A locked hotel room with him spread out on the bed is almost worth the alimony risk, if you know what I mean. Wattlesbrook can bring him back next time and I'd be hap-hap-happy. But if not, no big deal. He and Miss Heartwright are already engaged, and that's the fun part. I might like to try someone new next year and alter my character, become a bit more Elizabeth Bennet-y. You ended up with Nobley, didn't you? Is he a good kisser? He seemed tedious to me, but he did a good job of being into you. It was Nobley who asked me to pretend your cell phone was mine, you know. He said Wattlesbrook would send you home, asked me to do it as a favor. He was in my cast last year, too, and we nearly had a romance until George East swept me up. It was ill-fated at the time, of course, but that's half the fun. Ah, here we are! Such a tragedy when the vacation ends, but frankly, I'm dying for a massage."

While Amelia sprang out of the carriage and into the White Stag/Donkey, Jane sat a moment longer. The carriage still seemed to rock, but Jane was the one reeling. So, Amelia had been another

Miss Charming in disguise. Surely the actors thought Jane was the same as all the women visitors. And it'd been Mr. Nobley who'd saved her from expulsion. And . . . and . . . and it was over. Time to get out of the carriage and into her own clothes, meet up with Martin (hooray!), and be herself again. No more Mr. Darcy. Old Jane dead; new, confident, vibrant Jane rising from the oyster shell.

She sat in the inn's main room while Mrs. Wattlesbrook and Amelia had their last-day-of-school chat. Her bag was packed, all remnants of Miss Erstwhile were hanging back in the wardrobe. The old Jane would've stashed her ball gown, secretly imagining it could be her wedding dress if she married Martin. But the new Jane was set on just enjoying the early part and the memory of last night's kissing. The new Jane was still as self-possessed as she had allowed herself to be when she was Miss Erstwhile. It felt strange—and wonderful.

She was feeling sassy in her old street clothes, freshly laundered, bra and panties replacing corset and drawers. Jeans felt wicked to her, tight and strange, and yet so comfortable she hugged her knees to her chest. Wearing her own clothes gave her an eerie feeling, like the occasional moment when she glanced at herself in a mirror and had that frightening thrill of unrecognition. Is that who I am? That woman in the photographs, that's me?

And now, Who have I been for the last three weeks? Who am I now?

She looked around the room, remembering her first day when she'd danced the minuet there with Martin, how awkward and schoolgirlish she'd felt, how eager and afraid. She scarcely felt like the same woman anymore.

"Jane! Jane!" Amelia strode out of Mrs. Wattlesbrook's office and took Jane by the arms. "She told me of your financial situation . . . I'm so sorry! I didn't know." She embraced her and said quietly in her ear, "You hold on to your dreams, sweetie, you hear me?"

"I'll do that," Jane said, not caring to reveal that she'd come here to let her dreams go. She'd turned Mr. Nobley down, her trial in Austenland was over, and she was going home cleansed of entrapping fantasies.

Jane waited in Mrs. Wattlesbrook's office as the proprietress gushed farewells to her favorite Repeat Client. After Amelia (or "Barbara," as it turned out) was on her way, Mrs. Wattlesbrook brought in tea, and with undisguised disinterest, plied Jane with a satisfaction survey.

"And I trust you discovered a rewarding romance with one of the gentlemen?"

"Actually, there was someone, but, no, not one of the actors."

"Oh, well, of course you know that Martin *is* one of our own," Mrs. Wattlesbrook said.

What?

Clink as teacup was carefully replaced on its saucer.

"He's your gardener," Jane said slowly.

"Yes, but the servants are always prepared for an unexpected romance. We have discovered that not all our guests are able to relax and forget themselves enough to fall in love with the key actors, and so we have contingency plans. Besides, many women like to, how would you say, go slumming?"

Jane found herself blinking a lot and opening and closing her mouth. She felt as though she'd had the wind knocked out of her.

"Are you serious?"

"Oh, yes, he reported to me regularly. We knew of your fascination with basketball and the New York Knickerbockers, and the rest was easy."

"You are serious."

"You are not the first to fall for Martin," Mrs. Wattlesbrook said. "He is very good."

"Yes. Yes he is."

"We do not run a brothel here, miss, and I will have you know we would never let it go *that* far. I had to pull the plug on you two when Martin said things were spicing up, hm?" Mrs. Wattlesbrook smiled, and her eyes twinkled as if she enjoyed this part very much. "I wanted to make sure you knew that even though you are not our Ideal Client, we still made every arrangement possible for your comfort and entertainment, Miss Erstwhile."

"My name is Jane Hayes."

"There is a car waiting to take you to the airport, Jane Hayes. I trust you are ready to get on your way."

"I certainly am."

"I hope I have not upset you," Mrs. Wattlesbrook said with an innocent smile. "I pride myself on matching each client with her perfect gentleman. But one cannot anticipate a woman's every fancy, and so our talent pool runs deep. You understand?"

"Very deep indeed." Jane felt like a woman drowning, and she grasped for anything. And as it turned out, bald-faced lies are, temporarily anyway, impressively buoyant, so she said, "It will make the ending to my article all the more interesting."

"Your . . . your article?" Mrs. Wattlesbrook peered over her spectacles as if at a bug she would like to squash.

"Mm-hm," said Jane, lying extravagantly, outrageously, but also, she hoped, gracefully. "Surely you know I work for a magazine? The editor thought the story of my experience at Pembrook Park would be the perfect way to launch my move from graphic design to staff writer."

She had no intention of becoming a staff writer, and in fact the artist bug was raging through her blood now more than ever, but she just had to give Mrs. Wattlesbrook a good jab before departure. She was smarting enough to crave the reprieve that comes from fighting back.

Mrs. Wattlesbrook twitched. That was satisfying.

"And I'm sure you realize that since I'm a member of the press," Jane said, "the confidentiality agreement you made me sign doesn't apply."

Mrs. Wattlesbrook's right eyebrow spasmed. Jane guessed that behind it ran her barrister's phone number, which she would dial ASAP. Jane, of course, had been lying again. And wasn't it fun!

Mrs. Wattlesbrook appeared to be trying to moisten her mouth and failing. "I did not know . . . I would have . . ."

"But you didn't. The cell phone scandal, the dirty trick with Martin . . . You assumed that I was no one of influence. I guess I'm not. But my magazine has a circulation of over six hundred thousand. I wonder how many of those readers are in your preferred tax bracket? And I'm afraid my article won't be glowing."

Jane curtsied in her jeans and turned to leave.

"Oh, and, Mrs. Wattlesbrook?"

"Yes, Jane, my dear?" the proprietress responded with a shaky, fawning voice.

"What is Mr. Nobley's first name?"

Mrs. Wattlesbrook stared at her, blinkless. "It's J . . . Jonathan."

Jane wagged her finger. "Nice try."

Martin of Sheffield,

AGE TWENTY-NINE

He kissed her like she knew she was meant to be kissed. He smelled of gardens, tricked her brain into believing she was irresistible, and made the idea of falling in love seem possible again.

But really he was an actor posing as a gardener, who posed as a gentleman during balls in an Austenland estate where she'd gone to find out if she could let her fantasy of Mr. Darcy die at last. Seriously.

Also, he turned out to be a jackass.

the end of day 21

THE DRIVE TO THE AIRPORT felt eternal. Jane turned the backseat radio to a rock station and worked hard at being more angry than sad. Angry was proactive.

"Schmuck," she kept muttering. It was at herself.

Yes, Martin was a schmuck, too. The sheer certainty of that felt invigorating. But really, after all those boyfriends, you'd think she'd have learned that all men are schmucks.

It didn't help her humiliation much that she'd had no illusions about Martin. She knew that he'd just been a fling, motivated by her desperation to feel like a genuine woman amid the pageantry. But then she went and let herself get played. Stupid girl. She'd even convinced herself that Mr. Nobley might have been actually fond of her.

"Dream on," the radio crooned.

"It doesn't matter how it ended," she muttered to herself, and realized that it was true. Real or not, Martin had showed her that contented spinsterhood was not an option. And real or not, Mr. Nobley had helped her say no to Mr. Darcy. She leaned her head against the window, watched the countryside go whirling by, and forced herself to smile. Pembrook Park had done its job—it allowed her to live through her romantic purgatory. She believed now in earnest that fantasy is not practice for what is real—fantasy is the opiate of women. And she'd buried her fantasy behind her in the English countryside. Her life now would be open to real possibilities. There was no Mr. Darcy, there was no perfect man. But there might be someone. And she'd be ready.

The flight didn't leave for another two hours, so she wandered the airport, browsing bookshops and soap boutiques. She bought a best-selling paperback about a giant robot suit, found her gate, and was huddled in a vinyl chair trying to get past the first page when the congested voice of the loudspeaker called, "Miss, uh, *Erstwhile*, please report to the Terminal 3 Customer Service desk. Miss Jane Erstwhile to Customer Service."

The shock of that name zapped her, static electricity grazing her skin. She closed her book and stood up slowly, fearing to find

a camera crew crouched behind her, that she was the victim of reality TV and had been duped not privately but in front of millions
of viewers. She swung around, and the airport was full of disin-
terested bustle. In her present mood (chagrined and zippy mad), it
was hard to properly enjoy the relief that came with thinking, "At
least I'm not on TV."

The walk back past security felt impossibly long, the click of
her heels much too loud, as though she were all alone and no bodies were present to muffle the sounds of her solitude.

There was Customer Service, a chirpy brunette with a permanent smile behind the desk. And there was someone waiting
there, someone dressed in jeans and a sweater, devilishly normal in
the twenty-first-century crowd. He saw her, and he straightened,
his eyes hopeful. Apparently, Mrs. Wattlesbrook's barrister hadn't
been in his office to assure her that being a magazine writer
doesn't nullify a confidentiality agreement.

"Jane."

"Martin. You whistled?" She laid the rancor on thick. No
need to tap dance around.

"Jane, I'm sorry. I was going to tell you today. Or tonight. The
point is, I was going to tell you, and then we could still see if you
and I—"

"You're an actor," Jane said as though "actor" and "bastard"
were synonymous.

"Yes, but, but . . ." He looked around as though for cue cards.

"But you're desperately in love with me," she prompted him.
"I'm unbelievably beautiful, and I make you feel like yourself. Oh,
and I remind you of your sister."

The chirpy brunette behind the counter furiously refused to
look up from her monitor.

"Jane, please."

"And the suddenly passionate feelings that sent you running

after me at the airport have nothing to do with Mrs. Wattlesbrook's fear that I'll write a negative review of Pembrook Park."

"No! Listen, I know I was a cad, and I lied and was misleading, and I've never actually been an NBA fan—go United—but romances have bloomed on stonier ground."

"Romances . . . stonier ground . . . Did Mrs. Wattlesbrook write that line?"

Martin exhaled in exasperation.

Thinking of Molly's dead end on the background check, she asked, "Your name's not really Martin Jasper, is it?"

"Well," he looked at the brunette as though for help. "Well, it *is* Martin."

The brunette smiled encouragement.

Then, impossibly, another figure ran toward her. The sideburns and stiff-collared jacket looked ridiculous out of the context of Pembrook Park, though he'd stuck on a baseball cap and trench coat, trying to blend. His face was flushed from running, and when he saw Jane, he sighed with relief.

Jane dropped her jaw. Literally. She had never, even in her most ridiculous daydreaming, imagined that Mr. Nobley would come after her. She took a step back, hit something slick with her boot heel, and tottered almost to the ground. Mr. Nobley caught her and set her back up on her feet.

Is this why women wear heels? thought Jane. We hobble ourselves so we can still be rescued by men?

She annoyed herself by having enjoyed it. Briefly.

"You haven't left yet," Nobley said. He seemed reluctant to let go of her, but he did and took a few steps back. "I've been panicked that . . ." He saw Martin. "What are you doing here?"

The brunette was watching with hungry intensity, though she kept tapping at a keyboard as though actually very busy at work.

"Jane and I got close these past weeks and—" Martin began.

"*Got close.* That's a load of duff. It's one thing when you're toying with the dowagers who guess what you are, but Jane should be off limits." He took her arm. "You can't believe a word he says. I'm sorry I couldn't tell you earlier, but you must know now that he's an actor."

"I know," Jane said.

Nobley blinked. "Oh."

"So, what are *you* doing here?" She couldn't help it if her tone sounded a little tired. This was becoming farcical.

"I came to tell you that I—" he rushed to speak, then composed himself, looked around, and stepped closer to her so he did not need to raise his voice to be heard. The brunette leaned forward just a tad.

"I apologize for having to tell you here, in this busy, dirty . . . this is not the scene I would set, but you must know that I . . ." He took off his cap and rubbed his hair ragged. "I've been working at Pembrook Park for nearly four years. All the women I see, week after week, they're the same. Nearly from the first, that morning when we were alone in the park, I guessed that you might be different. You were sincere."

He reached for her hand. He seemed to gain confidence, his lips started to smile, and he looked at her as though he never wished to look away.

Zing, she thought, out of habit mostly, because she wasn't buying any of it.

Martin groaned at the silliness. Nobley immediately stuck his cap back on and stepped back, and he seemed unsure if he'd been too forward, if he should still play by the rules.

"I know you have no reason to believe me, but I wish you would. Last night in the library, I wanted to tell you how I felt. I should have. But I wasn't sure how you . . . I let myself speak the same tired sort of proposal I used on everyone. You were right to reject me. It was a proper slap in the face. No one had ever said no before. You made me sit up and think. Well, I didn't want to think much, at first. But after you left this morning, I asked myself, are you going to let her go just because you met her while acting a part?" Nobley paused as if waiting for the answer.

"Oh, come on, Jane," Martin said. "You're not going to buy this from him."

"Don't talk to me like we're friends," Jane said. "You . . . you were paid to kiss me! And it was a game, a joke on me, you disgusting lurch. You've got no right to call me Jane. I'm Miss Erstwhile to you."

"Don't give me that," Martin said. His patience was fraying. "All of Pembrook Park is one big drama, you'd have to be dense not to see that. You were acting too, just like the rest of us, having a fling on holiday, weren't you? And it's not as though kissing you was odious."

"Odious?"

"I'm saying it *wasn't*." Martin paused and appeared to be putting back on his romancing-the-woman persona. "I enjoyed it, all of it. Well, except for the root beer. And if you're going to write that article, you should know that I believe what we had was real."

The brunette sighed. Jane just rolled her eyes.

"We had something real," Nobley said, starting to sound a little desperate. "You must have felt it, seeping through the costumes and pretenses."

The brunette nodded.

"*Seeping through the pretenses?* Listen to him, he's still acting." Martin turned to the brunette in search of an ally.

"Do I detect any jealousy there, my flagpole-like friend?" Nobley said. "Still upset that you weren't cast as a gentleman? You do make a very good gardener."

Martin took a swing. Nobley ducked and rammed into his body, pushing them both to the ground. The brunette squealed and bounced on the balls of her feet.

"Stop it!" Jane pulled at Nobley, then slipped. He put out an arm and caught her midfall across her middle.

"Here, let me . . ." Nobley tried to give her a hand up and push Martin away at the same time.

"Get off me," Martin said. "I'll help her."

He kicked Nobley in the rear, followed by some swatting of hands. Jane planted her feet, grabbed Nobley's arm, and pulled him off. Martin was still swiping at Nobley from the ground. Nobley's cap fell off, then his trench coat twisted up around Martin, who batted at it crazily.

"Cut it out!" Jane said, pushing Nobley back and putting herself between them. She felt more like a teacher stopping a schoolboy scuffle than an ingenue with two brawling beaus.

"M-m-martin's gay!" Nobley said.

"I am not! You're thinking of Edgar."

"Who the hell is Edgar?"

"You know, that other gardener who always smells of fish."

"Oh, right."

Jane raised her hands in exasperation. "Would you two . . ."

A stuffed-up voice over the PA announced preboarding for Jane's flight. The brunette made an audible moan of disappointment. Martin struggled to his feet with a hand up from Nobley, and they both stood before Jane, silent, pathetic as wet dogs who want to be let back in the house. She felt very sure of herself just then, tall and sleek and confident.

"Well, they're playing my song, boys," she said melodically.

Martin's tall shoulders slumped as he sulked, and his long feet seemed clownish. Nobley had no trace of a smile now. She looked at them, side by side, two men who'd given her Darcy obsession a really good challenge. They were easily the most scrumptious men of her acquaintance, and she supposed she'd never had so much fun pursuing and being pursued. And she was saying no. To both of them. To all of it. Her skin tingled. It was a perfect moment.

"It's been a pleasure. Truly." She started to turn away.

"Jane." Nobley placed a hand on her shoulder, a desperate kind of bravery overcoming his reserve. He took her hand again. "Jane, please." He raised her hand to his lips, his eyes down as if afraid of meeting hers. Jane smiled and remembered that he really had been her favorite, all along. She stepped into him, holding both his hands down by her sides, and lightly pressed her cheek against his neck. She could feel him sigh.

"Thank you," she whispered. "Tell Mrs. Wattlesbrook I said tallyho."

She sauntered away without looking back. She could hear the men calling after her, protesting, reaffirming their sincerity. Jane ignored them, smiling all the way back through security, to the gate, down the jetway. Though pure fantasy, it was exactly the finale she'd hoped for.

She liked the way it had ended, had enjoyed her last line. *Tallyho*. What did that mean, anyway? Wasn't it like, *the hunt is on*, or something? Tallyho. A beginning of something. She was the predator. The fox had been sighted. It was time to run it down.

Okay, Aunt Carolyn, she said in a little prayer. Okay, I'm ready. I'm burying the wishful part of me, the prey part of me. I'm real now.

She snuggled into her seat and stared out the window at the dwarfish people on the tarmac, waving their orange-coned flashlights as though desperate to get her attention. She relaxed, and her mind wanted to puzzle over things. Which parts of Pembrook

Park had been real? Any of it? Even herself? The absurdity bubbled up inside her, and she laughed out loud. The woman next to her stiffened as if forcing herself not to look at the crazy person.

"Excuse me."

The sound of the voice flattened Jane against the back of her seat as though the plane had taken off at a terrifying speed.

It was him. There he was. In the plane. Vest and cravat and jacket and all.

"Holy cow," she said.

"Pardon me, ma'am," Nobley said to the woman beside Jane. "My girlfriend and I don't have tickets together, and I wonder if you would mind switching. I have a lovely seat on the exit row."

The woman nodded and smiled sympathetically at Jane as though pondering the sadness of a crazy woman dating a man in Regency clothes.

The man who was Mr. Nobley sat beside her. He lifted his hand to remove his cap, discovered it'd been dislodged during the scuffle with Martin, and then inclined his head just as Mr. Nobley would have.

"How do you do? I'm Henry."

So he was Henry Jenkins.

"I'm still Jane," she said. Or, squeaked, rather.

He was trying to fasten his seat belt and his look of confusion was so adorable, she wanted to reach over and help, but that wouldn't be in keeping with the . . . wait, they were on a plane. There were no more Rules. There was no more game. She felt her hopes rise so that she thought she'd float away before the plane took off, so she pushed her feet flat against the floor. She reminded herself that she was the predator now. Tallyho.

"This is a bit far to go, even for Mrs. Wattlesbrook."

"She didn't send me," said Nobley-Henry. "Not before, not

now. I sent myself, or rather I came because I . . . I had to try it. Look, I know this is crazy, but the ticket was nonrefundable. Could I at least accompany you home?"

"This is hardly a stroll through the park."

"I'm tired of parks."

She noticed that his tone was more casual now. He lost the stilted Regency air, his words relaxed enough to allow contractions—but besides that, so far Henry didn't seem much different from Mr. Nobley.

He leaned back, as if trying to calm down. "It was a good gig, but the pay wasn't astronomical, so you can imagine my relief to find you weren't flying first class. Though I'd prefer a cargo ship, frankly. I hate planes."

"Mr. Nob—uh, Henry, it's not too late to get off the plane. I'm not writing an article for the magazine."

"What magazine?"

"Oh. And I'm not rich."

"I know. Mrs. Wattlesbrook outlines every guest's financials along with their profiles."

"Why would you come after me if you knew I wasn't . . ."

"That's what I'm trying to tell you. You're irresistible."

"I am not."

"I'm not happy about it. You really are the most irritating person I've ever met. I'd managed to avoid any women of any temptation whatsoever for four years—a very easy task in Pembrook Park. Things were going splendidly, I was right on track to die alone and unnoticed. And then . . ."

"You don't know me! You know Miss Erstwhile, but—"

"Come now, ever since I witnessed your abominable performance in the theatrical, it's been clear that you can't act to save your life. All three weeks, that was you." He smiled. "And I wanted to keep knowing you. Well, I didn't at first. I wanted you to go away and leave me in peace. I've made a career out of avoiding any possibility of a real relationship. And then to find you in that circus . . . it didn't make sense. But what ever does?"

"Nothing," said Jane with conviction. "Nothing makes sense."

"Could you tell me . . . am I being too forward to ask? . . . of course, I just bought a plane ticket on impulse, so worrying about being forward at this point is pointless . . . This is so insane, I am not a romantic. *Ahem*. My question is, what do you want?"

"What do I . . . ?" This really was insane. Maybe she should ask that old woman to change seats again.

"I mean it. Besides something real. You already told me that. I like to think I'm real, after all. So, what do you really want?"

She shrugged and said simply, "I want to be happy. I used to want Mr. Darcy, laugh at me if you want, or the idea of him. Someone who made me feel all the time like I felt when I watched those movies." It was hard for her to admit it, but when she had, it felt like licking the last of the icing from the bowl. That hopeless fantasy was empty now.

"Right. Well, do you think it possible—" He hesitated, his fingers played with the radio and light buttons on the arm of his seat. "Do you think someone like me could be what you want?"

Jane smiled sadly. "I'm feeling all shiny and brand new. In all my life, I've never felt like I do now. I'm not sure yet what I want. When I was Miss Erstwhile, you were perfect, but that was back in Austenland. Or are we still in Austenland? Maybe I'll never leave."

He nodded. "You don't have to decide anything now. If you will allow me to be near you for a time, then we can see." He rested his head back, and they looked at each other, their faces inches apart. He always was so good at looking at her. And it occurred to her just then that she herself was more Darcy than Erstwhile, sitting there admiring his fine eyes, feeling dangerously close to falling in love against her will.

"Just be near . . ." she repeated.

He nodded. "And if I don't make you feel like the most beautiful woman in the world every day of your life, then I don't deserve to be near you."

Jane breathed in, taking those words inside her. She thought she might like to keep them for a while. She considered never giving them up.

"Okay, I lied a little bit." He rubbed his head with even more force. "I need to admit up front that I don't know how to have a fling. I'm not good at playing around and then saying good-bye. I'm throwing myself at your feet because I'm hoping for a shot at forever. You don't have to say anything now, no promises required. I just thought you should know."

He forced himself to lean back again, his face turned slightly away, as if he didn't care to see her expression just then. It was probably for the best. She was staring straight ahead with wide, panicked eyes, then a grin slowly took over her face. In her mind was running the conversation she was going to have with Molly. "I didn't think it was possible, but I found a man as crazy intense as I was."

The plane was moving, that scatty slow motion that seemed to go both forward and backward at once. Jane kept looking back and forth between the window and the man next to her, checking to see if he was really there. Was this a better ending than *tallyho*?

"So," he said, "is New York City our final destination?"

"That's home."

"Good. There's bound to be work for an attractive British actor, wouldn't you think?"

"There are thousands of restaurants, and those waiter jobs have high turnover."

"Right."

"Loads of theaters, too. I think you'd be wonderful in a comedy."

"Because I'm laughable."

"It doesn't hurt." On impulse, she took his hand, rubbed his index finger between her fingers. It was an intimate gesture, yet felt natural. What did she want? This is so insane . . . Stop thinking that. Maybe it could work . . . Oh, be practical, Jane. So what was she to do? She was no longer prey to the fantastical idea of love, but if she could have something real . . . Was there anything real?

"You want to have kids someday, don't you?" she asked, just to get that one out of the way.

"Did Mrs. Wattlesbrook tell you my story? I wouldn't be surprised. Yes, I like children. I always thought I'd like to be called Papa."

"Okay, that answer was too perfect. Are you honestly being you?"

"Wattlesbrook casts actors who are closest to the parts we play, since we had to stay in character so long. There are some exceptions, of course, like Andrews playing a heterosexual."

"I knew it," she said under her breath. "But wait, stop, it's not supposed to end this way! You're the fantasy, you're what I'm leaving behind. I can't pack you up and take you with me."

"That was the most self-centered thing I've ever heard you say."

Jane blinked. "It was?"

"Miss Hayes, have you stopped to consider that you might have this all backward? That in fact you are *my* fantasy?"

The jet engines began to whir, the pressure of the cabin stuck invisible fingers into her ears. Henry gripped his armrests and stared ahead as though trying to steady the machine by force of will. Jane laughed at him and settled into her seat. It was a long flight. There would be time to get more answers, and she thought she could wait. Then in that moment when the plane rushed forward as though for its life, and gravity pushed down, and the plane lifted up, and Jane was breathless inside those two forces, she needed to know now.

"Henry, tell me which parts were true."

"All of it. Especially this part where I'm going to die . . ." His knuckles were literally turning white as he held tighter to the armrests, his eyes staring straight ahead.

The light gushing through the window was just right, afternoon coming at them with the perfect slant, the sun grazing the horizon of her window, yellow light spilling in. She saw Henry clearly, noticed a chicken pox scar on his forehead, read in the turn down of his upper lip how he must have looked as a pouty little boy and in the faint lines tracing away from the corners of his eyes the old man he'd one day become. Her imagination expanded. She had seen her life like an intricate puzzle, all the boyfriends like dominoes, knocking the next one and the next, an endless succession of falling down. But maybe that wasn't it at all. She'd been thinking so much about endings, she'd forgotten to allow for the possibility of a last one, one that might stay standing.

Jane pried his right hand off the armrest, placed it on the back of her neck and held it there. She lifted the armrest so nothing was between them and held his face with her other hand. It was a fine face, a jaw that fit in her palm. She could feel the whiskers growing back that he'd shaved that morning. He was looking at her again, though his expression couldn't shake off the terror, which made Jane laugh.

"How can you be so cavalier?" he asked. "Tens of thousands of pounds expected to just float in the air?"

She kissed him, and he tasted so yummy, not like food or mouthwash or chapstick, but like a man. He moaned once in surrender, his muscles relaxing.

"I knew I really liked you," he said against her lips.

His fingers pulled her closer, his other hand reached for her waist. His kisses became hungry, and she guessed that he hadn't been kissed, not for real, for a long time. Neither had she, as a matter of fact. Maybe this was the very first time. There was little similarity to the empty, lusty making out she'd played at with Martin. Kissing Henry was more than just plain fun. Later, when they would spend straight hours conversing in the dark, Jane would realize that Henry kissed the way he talked—his entire attention taut, focused, intensely hers. His touch was a conversation, telling her again and again that only she in the whole world really mattered. His lips only drifted from hers to touch her face, her hands, her neck.

And when he spoke, he called her Jane.

Her stomach dropped as they fled higher into the sky, and they kissed recklessly for hundreds of miles, until Henry was no longer afraid of flying.

Henry

We met on an airplane (economy class) and kissed most of the flight home. Over the Atlantic, we decided to fall in love. When the plane touched down at JFK, he hadn't changed his mind. When he carried me over the threshold of my apartment, no Mrs. Wattlesbrook lurked in the shadows. While he was in the kitchen, I picked Pride and Prejudice *out of my (miraculously) still-living houseplant and tucked it into a harmless spot beside all the other DVDs, spine out and proud.*

We're going to order in tonight.

acknowledgments

HUGE THANKS, OBVIOUSLY, TO THE superhuman Jane Austen for her books. Besides those masterpieces, I also reviewed (obsessively) the BBC 1995 production of *Pride and Prejudice*, as well as *Emma* (1996), *Sense and Sensibility* (1995), *Persuasion* (1995), and Patricia Rozema's gorgeous revision of *Mansfield Park* (1999).

I'm also indebted to Daniel Pool's *What Jane Austen Ate and Charles Dickens Knew* for period information. *The World of Jane Austen*, by Nigel Nicolson, was also useful, and I scoured the Web site Jessamyn's Regency Costume Companion for clothing information. Despite the research, I'd be surprised if I didn't make mistakes, but they're sure to be my fault, so please don't blame my sources.

Special thanks to the amazing Amanda Katz for her inspired editing, as well as to Nadia Cornier, Cordelia Brand, Ann Cannon, Rosi Hayes, and Mette Ivie Harrison. And can I just say again how much I love Bloomsbury? I do. Everyone there is so cool. And also quite attractive (though that hardly seems fair, does it?).

And honey, you know that this Colin Firth thing isn't really serious. You are my fantasy man and my real man. I need no other fella in all the world besides you. It's just a girl thing, I swear.

Jane Hayes, a single graphic designer living in Manhattan, has a secret: she won't settle for anyone less than Fitzwilliam Darcy of *Pride and Prejudice*, that is, Colin Firth's Darcy in the BBC mini-series that she watches obsessively on DVD. Jane's great-aunt uncovers her little secret and bequeaths to Jane an all-expenses-paid trip to Pembrook Park, an "Austenland" for rich women looking to land an Austen hero. Jane hopes Pembrook Park will serve as immersion therapy—one last, luxurious swim in her Darcy obsession before she returns to the real world.

In Austenland, however, figuring out what is real (and what is clever acting) is even more confusing than the rules of whist. Torn between a sexy gardener and an actor playing the brooding Darcy role, Jane finds herself first mastering the etiquette rules, then reveling in her self-created role as the most beautiful girl at the ball. When it's time to bid Austenland goodbye, can Jane really leave her fantasies behind?

for discussion

These discussion questions are designed to enhance your group's conversation about *Austenland*, Shannon Hale's hilarious novel about one woman's drastic attempt to end her obsession with Mr. Darcy of *Pride and Prejudice* and her slow realization that fantasies do come true.

1. *Austenland* opens, "It is a truth universally acknowledged that a thirtysomething woman in possession of a satisfying career and fabulous hairdo must be in want of very little, and Jane Hayes, pretty enough and clever enough, was certainly thought to have little to distress her" (1). How does this sentence set the stage for the novel? Compare it to the famous first sentence of *Pride and Prejudice*: "It is a truth universally acknowledged, that a single man in possession of a good fortune, must be in want of a wife." Which of these universal "truths" is actually true, if either?

2. *Austenland*, besides chronicling Jane's stay at Pembrook Park, lists all thirteen "boyfriends" she's had in her lifetime. How well does the reader get to know Jane's past? How much has she changed from her first relationship at age twelve to the one that is now just beginning?

3. Jane observes of the BBC's *Pride and Prejudice*: "Stripped of Austen's funny, insightful, biting narrator, the movie became a pure romance" (2). What would *Austenland* be like without Jane's own funny, insightful, biting narration?

4. Looking at the gallery of portraits in Pembrook Park, Jane feels "an itch inside her hand" to paint a portrait, "but she scratched the

desire away. She hadn't picked up a paintbrush since college" (36). How is Jane's artistic itch intensified during her stay at Pembrook Park? How does she come to the realization that "she wanted to love someone the way she felt when painting—fearless, messy, vivid" (125)? In the end, has she found that type of artistic love?

5. In *Pride and Prejudice*, Elizabeth's mother, Mrs. Bennet, is known for her determination to marry off her daughters and for her frequent social blunders. How does Miss Charming, Jane's fellow visitor to Pembrook Park, resemble Mrs. Bennet? What are some of Charming's funny faux pas and verbal blunders?

6. Jane realizes, "Wait a minute, why was she always so worried about the Austen gentlemen, anyway? What about the Austen heroine?" (105) Is the heroine given short shrift by many Austen fans today? Why or why not?

7. Jane calls herself and Mr. Nobley "Impertinence and Inflexibility" (133). How do these nicknames originate? How do these traits compare to the pride and prejudice of Darcy and Elizabeth in Austen's novel?

8. Jane's great-aunt Carolyn set the whole Pembrook Park adventure into motion. What do you think Carolyn's intentions were in sending Jane to this Austenland? Do you think Jane fulfilled those expectations?

9. Jane comes to wonder what kind of fantasy world Jane Austen might have created for herself: "Did Austen herself feel this way? Was she hopeful? Jane wondered if the unmarried writer had lived inside Austenland with close to Jane's own sensibility—amused, horrified, but in very real danger of being swept away" (123). Is

it possible to guess at Austen's attitude toward romance by reading her work? Why or why not?

10. Looking at Henry Jenkins, Jane realizes that "just then she herself was more Darcy than Erstwhile, sitting there admiring his fine eyes, feeling dangerously close to falling in love against her will" (190). Are there other occasions in which Jane is more Darcy than Erstwhile? Is it possible that today's single, thirtysomething woman is more a Darcy than a so-called spinster?

11. Jane walks away from Nobley and Martin at the airport with the parting words, "Tell Mrs. Wattlesbrook I said tallyho" (186). Why does Jane enjoy her last line so much? What does she mean by "tallyho"?

12. What might Jane Austen think of *Austenland*, if she were alive today? Could she have possibly anticipated how influential her novels would become, even for twenty-first-century audiences? Could she ever have imagined a fan like Jane Hayes?

13. Shannon Hale reveals on her Web site (www.squeetus.com/stage/austen_journey.html) that the original title for *Austenland* was *Ostensibly Jane*, and that it evolved from a short story, to a novella, to a screenplay, to this novel. Can you imagine a shorter version of *Austenland*? A feature film? What would each be like?

14. Hale lists her "fantasy casting" of a movie version of *Austenland* at www.squeetus.com/stage/austen_casting.html. What is your own fantasy cast of *Austenland*? How does it compare to Hale's?

suggested reading

Jane Austen, *Pride and Prejudice*, *Emma*, *Sense and Sensibility*, *Mansfield Park*, *Northanger Abbey*, *Persuasion*; Karen Joy Fowler, *The Jane Austen Book Club*; Jon Spence, *Becoming Jane Austen*; Emma Campbell Webster, *Lost in Austen*; Laurie Viera Rigler, *Confessions of a Jane Austen Addict*; Amanda Grange, *Mr. Darcy's Diary*.